IN TUNE WITH ROMANCE

By

Patti Jo Moore

Published by Forget Me Not Romances, a division of Winged Publications

Copyright © 2019 by Patti Jo Moore

All rights reserved. No part of this publication may be resold, reproduced, stored in a retrieval system, or transmitted in any form or by any means, electronic, mechanical, recording, or otherwise, without the prior written permission of the author. Piracy is illegal. Thank you for respecting the hard work of this author.

This is a work of fiction. All characters, names, dialogue, incidents, and places either are the product of the author's imagination or are used fictitiously. Any resemblance to actual events, locales, or people, living or dead, is entirely coincidental.

ISBN-13: 979-8-8690-7321-1

DEDICATION:

Dedicated to my precious family and friends who continue to encourage and support me in my writing journey. With special love for Amy, Becca, Steven, and Eleanor---you've all made me very proud! Thank you also to my wonderful Publisher and my Editor---you are appreciated!

Most of all, I'm so thankful for my Lord and Savior Jesus Christ, who always puts a song in my heart. May my words always honor Him.

1

It was a tuna salad kind of day. Meg Mills needed comfort food, and she needed it fast. Although she would've preferred French fries, the salad would have to do. Doing her best to forget the phone call, she tried to focus on making the salad. She lifted a jar of mayonnaise from her refrigerator, but almost dropped it when her phone rang again.

Her best friend's voice came through, obviously worried. "Meg? I got out of the shower and read your text. Are you okay? How dare that woman call you and pretend to offer help." Zoey Hayes' indignation and loyalty brought a smile to Meg's face.

"I'm fine. It's predictable. Helena just wants the inheritance Roy left me."

Zoey practically snarled into the phone. "Oh, I bet she does. That woman isn't even blood-related to Roy, may he rest in peace. She was his stepmother—and they weren't even close."

Meg released a sigh. "Yeah, I know. It's sad because after his dad passed away Roy figured

Helena was a gold digger and had only married his father for the money. Then the next year when Roy died, things became crystal-clear."

"Well, don't let Cruella ruin your Saturday. Didn't you tell me at work yesterday you have some kind of appointment today?"

Meg grinned at Zoey's choice of names for Helena Mills and had to admit it was fitting. "Yes, I'm having my piano tuned today. But I'm making a bowl of tuna salad. Here's hoping my cottage won't smell too fishy when the piano tuner arrives." Reaching into her refrigerator again for the celery, Meg asked, "Are you and Trevor still going out for dinner this evening?"

Zoey released a huff. "We're supposed to, but with Trevor, I never know. He's likely to phone later today and tell me he needs to help his dad on a project. Sometimes I wonder why I keep dating him."

Not wanting to verbalize her thoughts that Zoey deserved better—which would only make her friend feel worse—Meg changed the topic. "Will you be in church tomorrow? We're singing some familiar hymns in the choir, so even though you had to miss practice, it won't be any big deal."

"Yes, I should be there, for sure. Did you let Mr. Randall know why I wasn't there for practice on Wednesday?"

Meg poured macaroni noodles into the pot of boiling water. "Yes, I told him you were having some allergy problems, and he said he hoped you're better soon."

"Okay, thanks. Bless his heart, Mr. Randall

does the best he can as our temporary choir director, but when is our church going to find a permanent replacement? It's late March, and it's been a while since the former director moved, right?"

"He and his wife moved close to Thanksgiving. That's when Mr. Randall started filling in. He does a good job, but you can tell he's only doing this to help out. We need someone who knows a lot about music."

Zoey agreed, then added, "I hope the church will hire someone talented and patient." She laughed again before reminding Meg of the many Sundays they'd arrived just in time to put their choir robes on. Although the elderly temporary choir leader never commented, he'd given the two young women a certain reprimanding look.

Meg's doorbell rang. "Must be the piano tuner. I'll see you at church tomorrow. Hope you'll have a fun evening with Trevor."

Meg hurried to open her front door, expecting to greet a middle-aged man, probably stocky and balding. But her eyes widened as she stared into the steel-gray eyes of a man who almost took her breath away. Yet for the life of her, she wasn't sure why.

~ ~ ~

Meg's mouth dropped open, and she must have had a deer-in-the-headlights look on her face. *This won't do,* she thought, *Get hold of yourself.* "Hello. Are you the piano tuner?" *Not at all what I expected.*

The tall, shaggy-haired man offered a shy grin

and nodded. "Yes, I'm Todd Davis." He awkwardly extended a hand toward Meg.

She hated when her heart raced, and she felt jittery—what was wrong with her? "Hi, I'm Meg Mills. Come on in." She stepped back and gestured toward the opposite wall in her living room. "I've recently inherited this from a great-aunt in Georgia. Well, actually her daughter had it, but didn't really want it, so I'm the lucky recipient." She grinned, not missing the almost-amused look on Todd's face.

He set his bag on the floor and lifted out tuning instruments.

"I know it's terribly out of tune, but I'm eager to brush up on my piano skills again and don't want to scare my cats, Georgia and Linus." Her hand covered her lips. "Oh my, I meant to ask you right away. Are you allergic to cats? I have two, but they'll stay hidden in my bedroom, I'm sure."

Todd's mouth curved into a halfway-grin and he shook his head. "No, I'm not allergic. I have a cat in my apartment." He returned his attention to his tools, so Meg took that as a gentle hint that she needed to allow him to get to work.

"Do you need anything to drink? I've got tea, coffee, and lemonade."

Todd shook his head, his brown bangs shifting a bit over his eyes. "No, thanks. I'm good." It was obvious the man was ready to focus on the piano, so Meg headed into her kitchen.

She'd forgotten all about her boiling macaroni, but thankfully reached her stove just in time. A couple more minutes and the pasta would've been scorched. All because she was chattering non-stop to a stranger—a stranger who for some reason was very appealing to her.

As the tuner worked, Meg continued preparing her tuna salad. The sounds from her extremely out-of-tune piano sounded even more pronounced as Todd worked, but Meg knew it would be wonderful to play her favorite hymns again without frightening her cats.

Thank goodness she'd made tuna salad so many times that it required very little thought on her part because her mind was definitely elsewhere. Todd Davis must be well over six feet tall, and although slender, he had a nice physique. His hair hung over his ears, a bit on the shaggy side, but not unkempt.

If she'd spotted him out somewhere, Meg would've assumed he was a basketball player rather than a piano tuner. Yet he didn't appear to be super athletic either. So why on earth did the man appeal to her?

In the past, Meg had usually gone for the more athletic or macho type. Not that her late husband had been athletic, but Roy had tried to present an outward masculine appearance, with his stocky build, choice of clothes, and pride in his motorcycle. Sadly, riding his motorcycle had ended his life.

Meg tamped down sad thoughts and put on a pot of coffee, hoping its rich aroma would cover the fishy smell of the tuna. A few minutes later she stepped to the doorway to see if Todd needed anything.

He shook his head, causing his bangs to cover

his eyes. "No, thanks. I should be finished in about twenty minutes."

"No rush. I don't have other plans today." *Oh great, why did I say that? I must sound like a pathetic loser.* She scurried back into her kitchen before she said something else she'd regret. Never at a loss for words, Meg tried to be considerate of others who weren't quite as talkative. And her piano tuner was certainly *not* talkative. Or maybe he was just shy.

Sitting at her kitchen table with a mug of coffee, Meg looked through recipes to get ideas for her family's Easter dinner. Hard to believe the special holiday was only a few weeks away. She needed to phone her mother soon and discuss the menu with her.

"I'm finished." Todd's deep voice startled her thoughts of recipes and family dinners. Meg hopped up from the table, almost spilling her coffee.

"Thank you so much. I've written a check and just need to fill in the amount. Are you sure you don't want something to drink? I've brewed a pot of coffee. Most people don't drink coffee in the afternoon, but I love it anytime."

He gave her the amount along with politely refusing her third offer of something to drink. She hurried to her kitchen table to fill in the amount, immensely relieved that it wasn't more. She'd prepared herself for this job to cost a small fortune, especially considering how out-of-tune the piano was.

After Todd placed her check in his pocket, he lifted his bag of tuning supplies and stepped to her door, then quickly turned around. "I almost forgot. Here's my card if you have any problems with your piano, but it should be fine."

Was he eager to leave? It wouldn't surprise her, given the fact she'd about talked the poor man's ears off. Yet for some reason she wanted to know more about him. "Have you lived in Coastal Breeze very long?" She braced herself for him to roll his eyes or make a mad dash to his car. Thankfully, he did neither.

"No, only about a month. My aunt lives here, and she encouraged me to come to Florida from Birmingham after my…my divorce." His face turned pink, and Meg had a crazy urge to reach out and hug him.

Instead, she held back her curiosity and asked about his aunt. When he told her his aunt was Ellen Davis, Meg squealed. "I know her from church. She is such a sweet lady. I'm sure she's happy to have a relative living here in the community."

Todd nodded, but remained silent.

"She must've put your business information on the church bulletin board. I was so happy to find a tuner in the area." She paused before adding another comment. "I've lived here for two years and love the Coastal Breeze church—everyone is so welcoming."

He nodded again. "Yes, I plan to start attending since that's where my aunt goes." He stepped onto her small front porch.

Enough with the chatter. "Thank you so much for tuning my piano. I can't wait to practice my hymns on it. Enjoy the rest of your weekend,

Todd." She flashed a cheerful smile at him, taking in his gray eyes that seemed to hold a secret. Or maybe it was the effects of getting over his divorce.

Minutes later, Meg sat at her piano, playing her favorite Easter hymn. The notes sounded so much better. Yet her mind was on the man responsible for tuning her piano. Maybe she'd see him the next day at church.

~ ~ ~

Pulling into his aunt's driveway, Todd knew he'd have to be careful not to mention Meg to his aunt. She'd likely try to play matchmaker, he was certain. And Meg Mills would never want to date an introvert such as himself. The phrase *never met a stranger* was likely how the woman's friends described her because she was certainly friendly. And talkative.

Before he'd climbed out of his car, his aunt stepped onto her small front porch to water her plants. She smiled and waved at him.

"Hello, Toddles." Using her affectionate nickname for Todd, the seventy-year-old set her watering can down, ready to grasp him in a hug. Ellen Davis was Todd's oldest aunt, and the only one who'd never married. She'd always claimed that no man could put up with her, although her family and friends adored her.

Todd had secretly wondered if she'd had her heart broken long ago and was determined never to go through that again. Well, he could relate, after the previous year.

He returned his aunt's hug, then remained on the porch while she continued watering her plants. "Are you sure you don't need me to pick up anything for you at the grocery store?"

"No, but you're always so kind to offer. I still enjoy getting out a few times each week and running errands, but it's comforting to know you're not far away." She winked at him, then gestured for the two of them to go inside.

Todd enjoyed visiting his aunt's cozy bungalow and being here made him yearn to hurry and get out of his apartment and have a house of his own.

"How was your piano tuning job?" Ellen bustled into her kitchen to check on something in the oven, so Todd followed her.

"It went well. I appreciate your spreading the word about my service to your friends at church, plus posting my information on the church bulletin board." He washed his hands and then poured himself a glass of iced tea. "Are you ready for your tea?" When his aunt nodded, he poured a glass for her and set it on the table.

Minutes later, the pair sat enjoying lasagna, salad, and garlic bread. Todd was hungrier than he'd realized. A comfortable silence hung in the air as they ate, until his aunt inquired about his other job.

"Are you still planning to continue with the substitute teaching assignment until the school year ends?" She spooned more salad onto her plate.

He nodded. "Yes, which should be in late May. Since the music teacher is on maternity leave, I'll finish out the year." He reached for another piece of garlic bread.

"I'm sure you'll find something you'll enjoy after that. At least you've got your tuning business to fall back on. You don't want to take on too much. You'll need to allow time for a personal life, in case you meet a special young lady." Her eyes twinkled.

Her comments caught him by surprise. "I'm hoping to do something else music-related, since that's where my heart is. And no worries, because no matter what I do I'll always have time to check on you and run your errands if needed." He took a swig of tea.

She reached over and patted his arm. "Oh honey, I wasn't thinking of you having time for me. I want you to have time for yourself. And a special someone." Her mouth curved into a wide smile, as if the very thought of her nephew finding true love made her happy.

Later, when he returned to his apartment, Todd thought back to his aunt's words. She'd referred to 'a special someone' as they'd visited, yet Todd couldn't help wondering if he would ever find someone special. With his first marriage, he'd honestly thought Tara was the woman for him. Boy, was he ever wrong about that. When they'd struggled financially—thanks to her love of shopping and extravagant spending habits—it had taken a great toll on their marriage.

He tried to keep his thoughts from dwelling on the past, but the impulse was strong to make sense of it all. Where had things gone wrong? As time went on, Tara became more and more dissatisfied, often complaining that her husband needed to find a job that paid more than his music teacher position at a Christian school near their home in Birmingham. She also disliked her job as a server in one of Birmingham's upscale restaurants, although her tips were usually quite sizable.

Attention that Tara received from some of the restaurant's male patrons didn't help the marriage, and before long his wife changed. It wasn't a big surprise when she announced she'd prefer to be single again.

A fresh pang of hurt, of failure seeped in. Was there something he could have done? She was basically an unhappy person, always looking for something to purchase that would raise her spirits.

A sigh came out. "Hi Mozart. Did you wonder when I'd be home?" Todd patted his gray-striped cat before hurrying to open a can of food for him. Then he put away the leftovers his aunt had insisted he take home. They'd come in handy for his meal tomorrow after church.

That night as he readied his suit and tie for the next morning, his mind returned to his tuning job earlier that day. With her long blonde hair and pretty face, Meg Mills was undoubtedly the most attractive client he'd ever met. But it wasn't only her appearance that had caught his attention. She was warm and welcoming, albeit more than a little talkative. He had the crazy feeling that it would've been easy to stay a while and visit with her.

Who was he kidding? Meg would've chattered on and on, and Todd would've been the proverbial stick in the mud, nodding and only speaking when she'd ask him a question. He was an introvert, and that's how God made him.

His quiet demeanor and tendency to appear withdrawn had been another factor in the dissolution of his marriage. Although Tara had clearly known she was marrying a shy man, after the wedding she continued trying to change him.

For some reason, Todd couldn't imagine Meg exhibiting some of the traits that Tara had, but he told himself that was a ridiculous thought. He'd only been around Meg once, and he knew basically nothing about her other than the fact she had two cats. Yet there was something about her that appealed to him—besides her physical appearance.

The fact that Meg mentioned having cats was a favorable sign, because his ex hadn't even liked animals. That should've served as a warning sign about Tara from the beginning, but Todd thought he was in love at the time. How wrong he had been.

~ ~ ~

The late March morning was overcast as Meg and Zoey hurried into the Coastal Breeze church. Meg was glad she'd remembered to stick her small umbrella into her handbag, as sudden rainstorms were common along the coast.

"Thanks again for swinging by to pick me up."

"No problem." Zoey grinned as they hurried to the back of the worship building to don their robes and join the choir. Mr. Randall smiled at the women as they took their places.

"It appears we're all here now, so I'll remind you of today's hymns." He quickly went over the list of hymns they'd sing, asked if there were any questions, and then led the group toward the choir loft.

As Meg took her place in the loft, she looked out over the congregation, feeling a warmth inside her as she gazed upon the friendly faces. To think that two years ago these people had been strangers, and now they were her church family. She was blessed to have located a caring church so close to her new home.

Joining the choir for the opening hymn, Meg smiled as she sang the familiar words of the beloved song. She knew the words and didn't need to look at her music, so instead her gaze swept the faces of the people seated before her. Just then a certain man caught her eye, and Meg's pulse quickened. *Todd Davis.* There was no mistaking the man making eye contact with her was her piano tuner.

Returning her gaze to her hymnal, Meg could feel her face redden. What was wrong with her? There was no need to feel flustered simply because she'd recognized her piano tuner, even if she did think he was attractive. *Focus on the service and the music,* Meg chided herself, but couldn't help but wonder if she'd have an opportunity to speak with Todd after the service.

When the morning service ended, Meg and Zoey hung their choir robes on hangers and headed toward the doors to exit. As usual, friendly church members spoke to them and thanked them for the choir's music. The women were headed to Zoey's car when Meg saw Todd walking ahead of them.

"Hello, Todd." Meg called to him. He immediately stopped, then headed toward them.

Zoey stuck out her right hand before Meg could make introductions. "Hello, I'm Zoey Hayes, Meg's best friend." She flashed a wide smile at Todd.

"This is Todd Davis, my piano tuner. By the way, you did a wonderful job. I played a few hymns yesterday and couldn't believe the difference. Before your tuning, I'd figured my playing had gotten really rusty." She shook her head and was relieved to see a slight smile on his face. Zoey kept her eyes directly on the tuner.

"I'm glad your piano sounds better." Todd spoke barely above a whisper.

A rumble of thunder sounded as church members scurried to their cars.

"Uh-oh, we better scoot. Nice to see you again, Todd. Have a good day." Meg smiled up at him again and then gestured toward Zoey's car, hoping her friend wouldn't continue gawking at the handsome man.

When the women climbed into Zoey's car, lightning zigzagged across the sky, followed by another loud rumble of thunder. Raindrops were sure to follow.

"Maybe we'd better just pick up our lunch and eat at my cottage if that's okay with you." Meg suggested as they exited the church parking lot.

Thirty minutes later the women sat at Meg's small kitchen table, enjoying their hamburger meals they'd gotten at a fast-food restaurant on the edge of

Coastal Breeze. Outside the cottage, thunder continued to rumble as the wind blew, making fat raindrops splatter against the windows. Meg's heart rumbled too when Zoey asked about Todd.

"Okay, so tell me about this piano tuner. He's super tall and cute. And he was at your house and you didn't tell me?" Zoey had a tendency to exaggerate in a playful sort of way, which always amused Meg.

Hoping her face wouldn't betray how attractive she actually found Todd Davis, Meg shrugged. "There isn't anything to tell, except now my piano sounds a hundred times better." She forced out a laugh before reaching for her tea. "I'm going to put on a pot of coffee. Will you drink a cup?" *Hmmm...that was an obvious change in topic*, but Meg didn't want to let her friend know how much she'd actually thought about Todd since he left her house yesterday.

Zoey eyed her curiously, then nodded. "Yeah, thanks. I'd love some coffee. But tell me more about this piano guy. I didn't notice a female with him—other than an elderly lady—so do you think he's single?"

Oh, good grief. Might as well tell Zoey the little bit she knew about him, because her friend could be quite persistent. Filling the glass carafe with water as she spoke, Meg made certain to keep her tone level.

"As I said, I don't know much about him at all. His aunt, Ellen Davis, encouraged him to move from Birmingham to Coastal Breeze after his marriage ended, and he likes it here so far. He lives in an apartment on the edge of town and he has a cat." She clamped her lips shut, bracing herself for her friend's scolding.

Zoey's eyes widened as she gathered up the trash from their meals on the table. "Girlfriend, you know a lot about him. And you didn't tell me? Sounds like he's single and ready for a new woman in his life." She playfully arched an eyebrow and placed a hand on her ample hip. "Since I've already got a part-time boyfriend, I'll give you first dibs on Mr. Piano Guy." She burst into giggles.

Her laughter was contagious and Meg found herself joining in. "A part-time boyfriend? Poor Trevor. Does he know he's referred to as 'part-time'?" Meg teased, silently hoping that something more permanent would work out for her best friend. Zoey and Trevor had dated for almost two years, and neither was getting younger.

Zoey nodded. "Until Trevor is ready to commit, he's considered part-time." She

released a long sigh. "I do hope he'll get serious before long, though. I want to have children, and I'm already thirty-two."

Meg's heart squeezed at her friend's words. How well she understood, because at thirty-one she also wanted children, and at the moment it didn't appear hopeful. Her phone rang before she could comment, so she grabbed it.

Her mother's voice came through. Meg knew if she didn't have Zoey over, she'd be in for an hour-long conversation. But that was okay because she and her mom were close. She excused her parents' overbearing ways because they loved her and wanted her to be happy.

A few minutes later the call ended, and Meg apologized to her friend. "Mom just wanted to discuss our Easter dinner plans. She said to tell you 'hello' and you're welcome to join us for our family dinner." Meg reached for two coffee mugs as she talked. The aroma of fresh-brewed coffee added a cozy feel to the cottage kitchen as the storm continued raging outside.

"Aww, that's so sweet. If I wasn't joining Trevor's family for Easter, I'd sure take her up on the offer." A shadow of sadness flitted over Zoey's features, and Meg knew she was thinking of her own parents, serving as missionaries out of the country.

Later that afternoon when the storm let up, Zoey headed to her home in Destin, and Meg jotted some ideas for Easter dinner recipes she'd try. But at the back of her mind, thoughts of a certain piano tuner hovered, and she had to admit she'd like to see him again.

~ ~ ~

2

Todd swung his car into a faculty space in the elementary school parking lot on Monday morning. The substitute teaching job in the Crestview area had been a godsend for him.

"Good morning, Todd. How was your weekend?" Darla, the school receptionist, greeted him as he entered the office to sign in. The scent of Darla's strong perfume caused his nose to itch, and he suppressed a sneeze.

"It was good, thank you." He didn't have a chance to inquire about her weekend, because the phone rang and a parent stepped to the counter, clutching a lunchbox a student had left at home.

Todd headed to the music classroom toward the back of the building, eager to look over that day's schedule of classes before the bell rang to begin the school day. He was thankful to have this temporary position, although it was a bit of a drive from his apartment. At least the traffic he encountered usually wasn't too heavy and it moved along, but driving wasn't his favorite thing to do.

Nope, music was pretty much his life. But he made the most of his driving time by listening to some of his favorite CDs—usually classical tunes or hymns.

His mind drifted to church the previous day, and how he'd thought about joining the choir. Seeing his lovely piano client, Meg Mills, in the choir was an incentive—not that Todd needed an incentive for anything music-related.

While preparing for that day's classes, Todd tried to stay focused but kept thinking of Meg singing with the choir. It was obvious her heart was in the music. Her face glowed as she sang. A fellow music-lover. Another reason the woman appealed to him.

"Good morning, Todd." A female voice coming from the classroom doorway startled him and he glanced up. One of the young teachers stood just inside the music room, grinning at him as she clutched a cup of coffee.

Trying to remember her name, Todd simply replied with "Good morning." He hoped she wouldn't linger to visit—after all, it was almost time for classes to begin.

"You're subbing a lot here, aren't you?" Was she batting her eyelashes at him, or was he imagining it?

He nodded. "Yes, I'm lined up to finish out this school year." His eyes darted between her and the lesson plans on his desk, hoping she'd get the hint and head to her own classroom.

To his relief, the bell rang, so the teacher had no choice but to scurry away toward her own classroom. Todd appreciated the employees at the school being cordial, but he had no intentions of becoming friends with any of them. Besides, this job was temporary, and then he'd likely never see any of these people again.

You're such an introvert. His ex-wife's words flashed through his mind. She'd often uttered that statement in an accusatory tone, as if being an introvert was akin to being a bank robber or serial killer.

Shoving his painful past from his thoughts, Todd stepped to the classroom door in order to greet the students as they entered. The second-graders bounded into the room, appearing pleased as they noticed Todd's presence. He assumed the regular music teacher did a good job, but he'd also heard she was quite strict, so apparently the students were enjoying Todd as their instructor.

The lessons went smoothly overall, and before he knew it, time was up and the students prepared to leave. As they lined up at the door, one of the girls looked up at Todd. "Mr. Davis, are you married?"

Todd should be used to unexpected questions by now from the young students, but he was still taken aback whenever one of the children tossed out a surprise question or comment. He shook his head. "No, I'm not." Then, before any other students had a chance to ask their own questions, Todd cleared his throat and spoke a bit louder. "Have a good day, boys and girls." He gestured for them to head back to their homeroom.

As he prepared for the next group of students, Todd couldn't help replaying the child's question. Would he ever reply differently to that question? He knew he was much better off single than being in an unhappy marriage as he'd been before. Still, there were times he longed for companionship—besides Mozart, the cat.

At the thought of his feline, Todd remembered that Meg had mentioned having two cats when he tuned her piano. That was something else they had in common. Yet she was so outgoing and friendly, so he assumed she'd likely prefer an extroverted man, not a quiet, shy man such as himself.

His musings were halted as the next class entered the music room, and Todd had to focus completely on the group of lively fourth-graders. But on his drive home that afternoon, his mind again returned to thoughts of Meg and how he'd like to know her better. Was it possible that might happen?

~ ~ ~

"Whew. What a week this has been." Zoey grinned at Meg as they prepared to leave the medical office where they both worked, Meg as the office manager and Zoey as a nurse.

"I know, but thankfully every week isn't this crazy. And at least today is Friday." Meg drew in a breath of the salt-tinged air drifting from the nearby gulf. As soon as she regained some energy, she'd enjoy a walk along the beach near her cottage.

When the women reached their cars, Meg called out to Zoey. "Enjoy your time with Trevor this weekend." She giggled as Zoey rolled her eyes in response. Secretly, Meg was thankful that Zoey's boyfriend wasn't available for dates every weekend, due to his job. That gave the two women some Saturdays each month to enjoy girlfriend time.

The late March sunshine poured into the window of her car as Meg drove the few miles to her cottage. But before heading to her street, she took a detour. Maybe her favorite gift shop was still open and she could browse for a few minutes. She swung into the small parking lot of Ginny's Treasures by the Sea, relieved to see the small OPEN sign still on the door.

The bell over the door gave a tinkling sound as Meg entered, and she was greeted by a refreshing citrusy scent. Ginny Grover, the gift shop owner, greeted her from behind the counter where she rang up sales for a customer. Meg had met Ginny the very first time she'd visited the shop, and liked the sixty-something woman right away.

Heading to the aisle with scented candles, Meg sniffed at a few before selecting one that smelled like gardenias. Although she'd enjoy browsing longer, it was about time for the shop to close, so she stepped to the counter to pay. The other customers were gone and Ginny had flipped the sign over to CLOSED.

"Am I keeping you late?" Meg quickly took out her wallet.

"Oh, sugar, no. You are welcome to keep looking if you need to. I've learned that if I don't go ahead and turn my sign over, I'll be here until midnight." Her southern drawl and easy laugh made Meg grin.

Before heading to the door, Meg paused as

Ginny commented about the church choir. "You always look so pretty up there in the choir loft. And I've noticed as you sing, your face just lights up." Meg blushed.

"You're very kind. I do love music, although I'm no professional singer." She laughed and slowly headed to the door. "But I'm glad you enjoy the choir's music."

"I sure do. Hearing the choir's music and Pastor Jack's preaching makes me look forward to Sunday mornings." She waved and told Meg to enjoy her weekend.

Meg continued her drive home, contentment filling her. Moving to Coastal Breeze two years ago had been the right thing to do. And hopefully the added distance from her late husband's stepmother would help Meg have peace of mind. She wasn't sure how much longer she could endure the woman's badgering phone calls, disguised behind the pretense of offering advice.

After arriving home and feeding her cats, Meg lit her new candle and prepared a sandwich for her supper. For some reason, her mind kept drifting to the previous Saturday when the piano tuner had been at her house and then seeing him after church on Sunday. She found him attractive, but didn't dare admit that to Zoey—at least not yet. With her friend's spunky personality, she was likely to march up to Todd and inform him that Meg was attracted to him. The very thought almost made her choke on her sandwich.

Her cell phone rang so she took a quick sip of tea before answering. Eve, Meg's mom, greeted her with excitement in her voice. "You're going to be an aunt again, Meg. Isn't that wonderful? Matt said I could go ahead and tell you."

Meg's pulse raced at hearing this news. Her brother, Matt, and his wife, Andrea, must be thrilled. She remembered how happy they were when little Spencer was born three years ago. "How exciting. That will be a good age difference between Spencer and the new baby. I'm so happy for Matt and Andrea." And she truly was—yet Meg couldn't deny the tinge of envy that poked at her and she hoped her mother didn't detect that in her tone. "When is the baby due?"

"Not until October, so Andrea has a while to go." Eve chuckled before chattering on about gift ideas if this baby was a girl. Yes, it was obvious that Meg's mother couldn't be happier to be a grandmother again.

After the call ended, Meg couldn't ignore the yearning that hovered deep inside her heart. She'd been married once, but before she'd been blessed with any children, her husband died. Would she ever have another chance? Another marriage that would be blessed with children?

Although she tried hard not to focus on that yearning, it was always there. She couldn't deny it, so she tried to keep it hidden as she expressed her happiness for other couples—especially her brother and his wife.

Determined to move her focus off her own feelings, she decided to begin work on a gift for her sister-in-law. Since Meg enjoyed doing cross-stitch, she'd create a cute print that could be for a boy or girl, since they didn't yet know the baby's gender.

As she gathered her stitching supplies, her mind buzzed with anticipation as she visualized a nursery-rhyme print she could do, and minutes later she was absorbed in her task. To her surprise, her mind switched gears as she again thought back to the previous Saturday. Images of the lanky, somewhat shaggy-haired man who worked on her piano hovered in her thoughts. At least thinking of him was a pleasant diversion.

~ ~ ~

Having a relative who'd lived in Coastal Breeze for a few years had proven to be a big help to Todd—especially where tuning jobs were concerned. It amazed him how many people his aunt knew and also how many of those were piano-owners. Thanks to Aunt Ellen, Todd had tuning appointments lined up for the next few weekends, which was a good thing, since he basically had no social life these days.

After finishing a job in the Destin area on Saturday morning, he pulled into a grocery store parking lot. Ugh. He didn't particularly enjoy shopping, and Saturdays were usually busy in the stores, but he had no choice. Mozart was low on cat food, and even if Todd went without something, he wouldn't let his cat go hungry.

Just as he'd expected, the store bustled with shoppers of various ages, including moms with young children in tow. He passed a couple with twins, who appeared to be around six. They made a cute family, he had to admit. Would he ever have children? His ex-wife had announced *after* their marriage that she really didn't care to have a family. That had been a shocker to him and only one of many factors leading to their split.

Focus on your list. He chided himself as he pushed his shopping cart down the pet food aisle. About ten feet ahead of him, eyeing the cans of cat food, stood the lovely client from last week, Meg Mills. Without meaning to, Todd stopped short and stared.

She glanced up and a smile lit her face. "Hi there. Am I in your way? Just trying to decide which kinds of food to buy for my finicky felines." A lilting chuckle followed her words, and she shook her head. "I know it's my fault that they're so picky because I do spoil them." She stepped to her left to allow Todd some space.

He pushed his cart closer, parked it, then joined her at the shelves of cat food. "Yeah, I know what you mean. Mozart is pretty pampered himself." He grinned, hoping he didn't appear as awkward as he felt.

Meg glanced up. "I love your kitty's name—Mozart. And how appropriate since you're a piano tuner." Her blue eyes held his gaze for a few moments, and Todd realized he'd better say something sensible or he'd stand there gawking at her. What was it about this woman?

He nodded. "Yeah, the name came to me right away after I adopted him at a shelter. He's a good companion." Oh boy, did that make him sound like a pathetic, lonely guy?

But to his surprise, Meg's eyes held a look of compassion, as if she completely understood. Then she spoke in a softer tone, "Yes, I've never understood people who don't love cats as I do. Cats are such comforting pets, and I love the fact they're self-sufficient." She hesitated before giggling. "Mainly the fact that they use a litter box and don't have to be taken outside at certain times." A rosy hue crept up her face.

Todd nodded. "Oh yeah, that's a big plus about having a cat." He reached for some cans of food, wondering how long their conversation might continue. He'd like to keep chatting with her if only he didn't feel so awkward. He used to blame it on his lankiness, but finally realized it was just his personality.

As he continued reaching for cans of food, Meg did the same. At one point their hands brushed and they both jerked away.

"Someone might see us and think we're fighting over cat food." She spoke lightly and gave him a teasing grin. Something about the way she looked up at him sent his stomach doing flips. A sensation he'd not experienced in a very long time.

Moments later they headed away from the pet food, but before exiting the aisle with her shopping cart, Meg offered a sweet smile over her shoulder. "It was nice to see you again, and I hope Mozart is pleased with his food."

Todd offered a weak thanks. Good grief. Why couldn't he act more relaxed around this woman? She probably thought he was a recluse who only went out to tune pianos and buy cat food. No, she'd seen him at church, so at least she knew he went there, too.

As she disappeared around the corner, Todd sniffed in a fresh, floral scent that lingered behind. An appealing scent—just like the woman. Was he becoming more attracted to her? She was widowed, but most likely someone like Meg Mills had another romantic interest. Probably someone outgoing—unlike himself.

Ten minutes later Todd stood in line at a check-out and glanced over to his right just in time to see Meg paying for her groceries in another line. As their eyes met, she held up a hand in a discreet wave. The simple, casual gesture sent Todd's stomach into somersaults—yet again. He wasn't sure how to handle the feeling.

~ ~ ~

Meg finished her salad and soup, then began work on the cross-stitch print for her brother's expected baby. Ever since going to the grocery store earlier in the day, she'd not been able to keep her thoughts off of Todd Davis. What was it about the shaggy-haired piano tuner that held appeal for her? He certainly didn't appear to be the macho or athletic type, yet there was something in his eyes that went straight to her heart.

He'd mentioned his marriage ending, so that had likely been painful for him. Poor guy. A wave of sympathy took hold of Meg's thoughts. Yet she had no idea of his marriage details, so she shouldn't judge his ex-wife. But from the little she'd seen of

Todd during the few times she'd been around him, the man seemed gentle and kind. So unlike her late husband.

Guilt poked her at that thought, but it was the truth. Although she'd loved Roy, he had proven to be quite a different man after they'd married. His temper flared at times, and his fondness for alcohol didn't help matters. Still, Meg had tried her best to be a loving wife and practiced patience with Roy. Now, if only his stepmother would leave her alone. A shudder ran up Meg's spine at the thought of Helena Mills. Or as Zoey referred to her—Cruella.

Meg's cell phone rang, and she grabbed it up, amazed when she saw Zoey's name on the caller ID. She answered with a giggle, "Zoey, you won't believe this. I was just thinking about you."

"Well, I hope it was a good thought." Her friend's voice held teasing.

"Of course. But unfortunately, I was thinking of Roy's stepmother and your nickname for her."

"Ah, you mean Cruella. Has the wicked woman caused you more grief?"

"None lately, thank goodness. I'd better knock on wood." Meg reached out and tapped her coffee table. "I'm surprised to hear from you since it's Saturday night. I thought you and Trevor had a date."

An exasperated sigh greeted Meg's ears before her friend expounded on her boyfriend's change of plans. "Yeah, well, we went bowling this afternoon and had planned to eat out tonight. Then he got sick supposedly from the snacks he enjoyed at the bowling alley. Anyway, here I am—at home on

Saturday night. No big deal. What are you doing? Besides thinking of Cruella." Zoey's serious tone dissolved into laughter.

Meg updated Zoey on the family's expected baby in October, the cross-stitch gift she was working on, and then told her about stopping at the local gift shop the previous day. "You know, it just occurred to me that Ginny's Treasures by the Sea also carries baby items, so I'll have to look at those next time I stop by."

Although Meg hadn't expressed her private thoughts about wondering if she'd ever have a baby for her family to celebrate, somehow Zoey seemed to discern her feelings.

"I'm sure you're happy for your brother and his wife. But I have a feeling one day they'll all be excited when *you* announce a little one on the way."

"Oh Zoey, you're such an encouraging friend. But there's one minor detail you didn't mention."

"You mean the guy? Yeah, there will be a wedding before your announcement, I'm certain. So now all we gotta do is locate one for you. But who am I to play matchmaker? I can't even get my own boyfriend to commit." An underlying resentment colored Zoey's words, so Meg changed the topic.

"Will you be at church tomorrow morning? If so, I'll see you in the choir loft. Maybe I can actually arrive before they're warming up." Meg knew she really needed to get an earlier start on Sunday mornings, but by the time she did cat-related duties and got herself ready, the clock always seemed to jump ahead.

Zoey assured her she'd be there and would

look for her. The friends chatted a few more minutes and the call ended.

As Meg resumed her stitching, her mind drifted back to Zoey's comments about Meg's future. She appreciated the encouraging outlook her friend had. If she remarried one day, Zoey would be her maid of honor.

But the main—and biggest—question loomed in her mind. Who would be her groom? To her astonishment, the lanky piano tuner again made an appearance in her thoughts.

~ ~ ~

Another piano job lined up—a good sign for Todd's finances. After all, his current teaching job would be ending in less than two months, and he had no future plans securely in place. Any extra funds would be helpful.

Thankful he'd purchased a map of the Florida panhandle when he'd first moved there, Todd kept it handy in his car so he wouldn't be late for an appointment. He knew his way around Coastal Breeze, which was small, but some of the nearby towns were still foreign to him.

On Saturday morning he'd loaded up his tuning supplies, grabbed a bottled water, and drove from his apartment to the town of Crestview. Although his car had a GPS, Todd preferred a paper map and always made certain to plan his route ahead of time. However, after making several turns, he wondered if he'd need to rely on his GPS after all.

To his relief, he reached the road he'd been

searching for and made a right turn, looking for house numbers on mailboxes. He noticed in this particular area the houses were spaced further apart and it appeared the homeowners had more land. About a mile after turning onto the road, he spotted the number on a mailbox. Good. And he still had a few minutes to spare, because he made sure to never arrive late.

As he turned into the driveway, Todd froze. His foot applied the brake as his heart pounded. The large, older house looked to be well-maintained and was situated a good distance back from the road. A charming, inviting place, but it wasn't the house that made him stop; it was the lake in front of it. His fingers gripped the steering wheel and his foot remained on the brake. *Just drive. You have an appointment.* The silent self-talk urged him forward very slowly.

Why did there have to be a lake on this property? And not simply a lake, but one that closely resembled the one from his past. Too similar.

He knew he must calm himself before going to the door or the client might think he was sick. Physically or mentally. Shutting off his car engine, Todd took a few swigs of his water, thankful it was still cool from being in his refrigerator.

With the angle of his parked car in the client's driveway, the lake was now visible in his rearview mirror. He mustn't look. Grabbing the sheet of paper from the passenger seat, Todd looked over the information he'd jotted. This client was a woman related to someone who knew his aunt, and according to what she'd said over the phone, her piano hadn't been tuned in over five years. Although he hadn't seen her yet, her voice sounded middle-aged.

The front door opened, and a dark-haired woman stepped onto the front porch and waved. She must wonder why he was still sitting in his car. Todd returned the wave before slowly getting out. After hoisting the bag of tuning supplies onto his shoulder, he headed toward the waiting client, thankful the lake was now completely out of his view.

"Hello, you must be Todd. I'm Susan Hancock, and my sister, Vickie Russell, knows your dear aunt. Did you have trouble locating my house?" The middle-aged woman stepped back to allow him entrance to her home.

"No, ma'am. I found it with no problems." *Until I saw your lake.* Todd knew he must stay focused on the job he was there to do.

Susan Hancock led him to her piano in the next room. With a sweeping gesture she indicated her numerous figurines and knickknacks placed here and there on tables and shelves. "I'm a collector, and normally my piano is also filled with my little odds and ends, but I moved everything so nothing would be in your way." She beamed at him.

Todd nodded politely as he couldn't help feeling relief that she'd moved the fragile-looking items. He'd feel terrible if he accidentally knocked something off the piano and it broke. Not that he was usually clumsy, but with his height, things sometimes happened.

"Would you like something to drink?"

"No, thank you. I'll just get started on your piano." He appreciated her hospitality, but wanted to complete this job and leave. *And get away from that lake.*

About two hours later, Todd had completed the tuning, and his client seemed pleased. He packed away the tuning hammer, screwdriver, and his other equipment, thanked her when she handed him a check, and headed to the door.

Susan followed him to the door, making small talk about the temperatures getting warmer and relatives visiting in the summer. Then her talk turned to the lake on her property. "That lake has been a blessing and a curse." She paused and laughed. "We enjoy looking at it, but when my young grandkids are here visiting, we have a challenge. Someone has to be with them constantly to make certain they don't fall in. They always want to stand at the edge and peer into the water."

Todd's pulse raced and his right hand tightened on the handle of his equipment bag. All he could do was listen without replying. The woman had no idea how the innocent comments about her lake were affecting him. How could she?

With a forced smile and a nod, Todd again thanked her for using him to tune her piano, told her to enjoy her weekend, and hurried to his waiting car. He kept his eyes trained only on his vehicle. With a breath of relief, he heard the door close behind him, so there was no chance of more conversation. Now to exit this property and return to the confines of his apartment.

Driving off the client's land, Todd kept his gaze fixed on the driveway in front of him, but with his peripheral vision he couldn't help seeing a portion of the lake. He gripped the steering wheel tighter and stomped the gas pedal. He knew if Susan Hancock was watching from her window, she'd wonder what on earth was wrong with him—speeding out of her driveway like a madman.

Yet once on the main road again, Todd couldn't deny the overwhelming sense of relief that washed over him. Who would think that someone living right at the beach would have a problem with lakes? But for him, that's the way it was. All due to his past and the painful memories he couldn't shake.

3

Easter Sunday arrived sunny and warm, making the early-morning drive to her parents' home pleasant. Although Meg hated missing the worship service at her own church in Coastal Breeze on this most special of Sundays, she wanted to be with her family in Panama City. She also knew how much it meant to her mother when she was able to have all the family with her in their church.

Pulling into the driveway of her parents' modest stucco home, Meg was relieved to see she wasn't late, according to the clock in her car. She glanced up to see her mother at the door, smiling and waving.

"Hi, Mom. Happy Easter." Meg hugged her mother before unloading the food she'd brought. "The deviled eggs need to go in the refrigerator, but everything else is fine to stay out on the counter until we eat." She didn't miss the pleased look on her mother's face. Meg secretly hoped her siblings also brought their share of food, because she worried about these family meals being too hard on her mother.

"The others are meeting us at the church, so we can head on if you're ready." Her mother grabbed her handbag, then called to Meg's father that it was time to leave.

Minutes later Meg sat with her parents, sister, brother, and their spouses as the church choir sang a beautiful Easter medley. She was filled with a sense of peace and contentment, thinking of the wonderful Easter message in the words of the music. She only hoped these good feelings would continue once the family gathered to eat at her parents' home. Sometimes well-meaning family members offered unsolicited advice, and Meg didn't want to hear any today.

Back at the house, Meg's father offered a blessing before everyone loaded up their plates. Meg's deviled eggs, green-bean casserole, and peach cobbler garnered more than a few compliments.

"Since you're such an awesome cook, you'll be married again in no time." Her brother Matt teased her before his wife commented about adding more babies to the family. Matt piped up again. "Yeah, Spencer and his sibling will need some cousins."

They meant well, but today she wasn't in the mood for their comments. As if sensing her thoughts, Meg's sister, Marissa, leaned over to her and whispered, "You're still young, Sis, so you don't need to be in a hurry."

After giving her sister an appreciative nod, Meg changed the topic by inquiring about Matt's expected baby. "When will you learn if it's a girl or boy?"

His wife answered with excitement shining in her eyes. "In about six weeks, and I can't wait. We'll be thrilled either way, but I'll be glad to know whether to prepare for a girl or a boy."

An unexpected yearning welled up inside Meg as she observed her sister-in-law placing a protective hand on her stomach. It was obvious she was just as thrilled about her second pregnancy as she'd been about the first.

Throughout the afternoon, the family continued visiting, and after Spencer's brief nap, they all enjoyed playing with the lively toddler. It was cute to hear his attempts at saying Meg's name as it came out sounding more like 'egg' than Meg. She genuinely loved her little nephew and looked forward to welcoming another nephew or niece. Yet the yearning remained, and without a doubt she wanted a child of her own.

"Hey, Aunt Egg." Her brother snapped his fingers in front of her face, a teasing glint in his eyes. "Where were you? Zoning out on your family?" He laughed good-naturedly, but heat rushed up her face. She absolutely must not let her family know about her yearnings, or they'd go overboard attempting to play matchmaker and encouraging her to date.

She playfully jabbed her brother's shoulder. "How could I zone out in this family?" She giggled and shook her head before listening to her brother's latest joke. He was definitely the family ham whenever they gathered.

Later that day, Meg hugged them all before driving back to Coastal Breeze. She'd enjoyed being with her family, but was unprepared for the comment her sister-in-law whispered to her before she headed out the door. "Maybe before long you'll have a special someone at these family get-togethers." She smiled sweetly and winked, but all Meg could do in response was nod.

Yes, they meant well. But she didn't want sympathetic matchmakers—no matter how good their intentions. After Roy had died, Meg had received overwhelming sympathy and acts of kindness bestowed on her, which she greatly appreciated at the time. But she'd gotten stronger and moved on, and if and when she had a romantic interest in her life, she wanted it to come naturally. Not from someone's pity over her status as a widow.

After all, she couldn't deny the fact she was a widow. But she did her best to keep the loneliness at bay, and so far, was doing a pretty good job. Her thoughts were interrupted as her cell phone rang, but she didn't like to talk while driving. As soon as she'd pulled into her driveway, she checked the caller ID and saw Zoey's name.

Meg entered her house, fed her cats, and put away the few leftovers she'd brought home before phoning her friend. "Hi Zoey, are you having a nice Easter?"

"Hey Meg, I was worried when you didn't answer. Yep, it's been nice, and I actually got to spend some time with Trevor." She offered a forced laugh. Her friend tried to keep a good attitude about her less-than-attentive boyfriend.

"Sorry you were worried, but I was driving back from my parents' home and decided to wait until I was home to check my phone. I'm glad you had a good day and hope you didn't eat as much as I did."

After a few more minutes of general chit-chat, Zoey explained the reason for her call. "I know I'll see you at the office tomorrow, but sometimes the day after a holiday is super busy, so I wanted to go ahead and ask about this now." She hesitated. What was her friend worried about?

Zoey blew out a sigh. "Did you hear from Cruella today? I was hoping she didn't have the nerve to bother you on a special holiday, although she's done so in the past, claiming she was missing her stepson." Zoey released a sarcastic snort.

"No, I didn't hear a thing from her. Which is a blessing. To be honest, even if she'd phoned me while I was with my family, I probably would've ignored her call. I wish she didn't have my phone number."

"Yeah, but remember if she bugs you too much, you can always get a new number."

Zoey was looking out for her and she was grateful for such a devoted, caring friend. But she also knew that she mustn't allow her obviously disturbed former mother-in-law to bother her, no matter how often the woman was in contact.

"Thanks for your concern. It really means a lot. I'm just thankful she lives two hours away and not here in Coastal Breeze." A shiver ran down Meg's spine at the thought of encountering Helena Mills frequently, as she'd be likely to do in her small community.

After the call ended, Meg prepared her uniforms for the upcoming work week and thought about Zoey's concern and friendship. Meeting her at the medical office where they both worked had been a huge blessing in Meg's life, and from all indications, her friend felt the same way. She knew how badly Zoey wanted to marry, and Meg hoped Trevor would become serious in the near future. Or if he wasn't the one for her friend, that Zoey would meet Mr. Right before long.

Who knows? Maybe things would work out so she and Zoey would both be planning weddings around the same time. Without any prompting, the image of Todd formed in her mind. And with the image, a tingling feeling coursed through her. Good grief, how could she be so drawn to a man she hardly knew?

~ ~ ~

Todd had been surprised when he hadn't seen Meg in the church choir on Easter Sunday morning. Okay, he'd also been disappointed, too. He hoped she wasn't sick, but decided maybe she was with relatives. *Or a boyfriend who lives out of town.* The unbidden thought bothered him more than he cared to admit, so he shoved it aside and focused on the meaning of the special day.

Aunt Ellen had prepared several dishes and invited a few friends to join her and Todd. Although he felt like a youngster among the older folks, he enjoyed himself and the scrumptious meal.

One of the women who joined them was Midge Weatherbee, an outspoken but kind-hearted woman who wore bright lipstick and always chimed in with her opinion on a topic. While enjoying dessert, she paused between bites and smiled pointedly at Todd. "Do you have a special lady friend, Todd?"

He didn't miss the look his aunt shot him, as though silently apologizing for her friend's question. Yet he didn't mind because he'd already learned that Midge said pretty much what was on her mind.

Shaking his head, he smiled and told her that he didn't.

"Well, a handsome young man such as yourself won't remain single very long, I feel certain." Midge beamed at him before taking another bite of her lemon pie.

Aunt Ellen quickly piped up with comments about the beautiful Easter lilies that had adorned the church altar that morning, which prompted the conversation to turn to plants.

Todd busied himself pouring coffee for everyone and was relieved when Midge moved on to a new topic. He secretly hoped that she or any of his aunt's other friends wouldn't attempt to play matchmaker. Besides, he needed to focus on work and finances, rather than looking for a romantic relationship.

After the guests left, Todd stayed to help his aunt clean the kitchen. "Everything was delicious, but I'm afraid I ate too much." His aunt enjoyed seeing folks eat, and his praise for her food brought a smile.

"I'm glad you enjoyed Easter dinner, Toddles, and there's plenty of leftovers for you to take home. Including some ham for Mozart." She added with a twinkle in her eyes. "I hope Midge's well-meaning comments didn't bother you. She's known for trying to connect people—whether in a romance or just in friendships."

"No, I think I've already learned how Midge Weatherbee is, so no worries." He closed the dishwasher after loading the last plate. But eyeing his aunt, he knew she was about to say more.

"Well, I will admit that I'll be happy when you find a special someone. You deserve so much better than how Tara treated you. I hate to say this, but she was extremely self-centered and didn't deserve you." Ellen clamped her lips together and grabbed the dishcloth. Her vigorous swipes of the counter let Todd know his aunt was trying to control her comments about his ex.

He patted her shoulder. "Thank you. You've always been my biggest encourager, and it means a lot. But Tara is in the past and I'm much better off now. If there's someone out there for me, the Lord will show me."

Ellen gazed up at him with tenderness in her eyes. "Oh, Toddles. I'm so proud of you and love you like a son." She paused and then giggled. "I guess you could say you're the son I never had." She placed the dishcloth on the counter and squeezed his arm.

A lump formed in his throat and he willed himself not to become emotional. He knew his aunt loved him, but he hadn't realized until that moment how much. Trying to lighten the mood, he glanced around the kitchen. "Okay, what else can I do before I deliver ham to Mozart?" He chuckled and was glad to see his aunt grinning.

"Not a thing. In fact, you were very kind to stay and help me. Now I can enjoy reading for the remainder of this lovely Easter."

Twenty minutes later Todd was in his apartment, feeding small bites of ham to Mozart. Yet his mind drifted to the earlier comments made by Midge Weatherbee during dinner. He replayed her well-meaning words about finding a special someone. Had that train passed or was there still a chance, maybe even in Coastal Breeze?

~ ~ ~

As Todd exited the school parking lot Tuesday afternoon, his cell rang. His aunt's raspy voice concerned him. "Aunt Ellen, are you sick?" If not for seeing her name on his caller ID, he would've thought it was a wrong number.

A weak chuckle preceded her words. "It's just a sore throat and cough, Toddles. I'll be okay. But would you mind terribly going by the store and picking up a bottle of cough syrup for me?"

"No, I don't mind at all. Tell me what else you need, and I'll get it for you. Soup? Orange juice?" He tried to think of anything that might appeal to his aunt.

"Just cough syrup will be fine, dear. I have everything else I need. Thank you so much." A coughing spell ensued, so he assured her he'd be there as soon as possible.

Concern filled him for his aunt. Elderly folks often didn't recover from sickness as easily as younger people. The fact that his aunt had even phoned him to stop by the store was an indication that she felt poorly.

Todd hurried through the store, grabbing a few extra items she might need, including soup, juice, and a box of tissues. Relieved the store wasn't crowded, he was out of there within minutes.

When he arrived at her house, Ellen greeted him at the door, clasping a tissue and looking up at him with watery eyes. "Oh, you're the best. What would I do without you?" She released a weak chuckle. "When I encouraged you to move to Coastal Breeze, it wasn't so you could be my errand boy." She grinned at him, then a fresh round of coughing began.

"I would never think that, and I want you to phone me anytime you need anything." Todd showed her what he'd brought from the store, and her reaction pleased him. When she tried to pay him, he refused. After all his aunt had done for him—especially after he'd lost his parents in the accident—there was no way he'd allow Ellen to pay him for a few store items.

He didn't want to let on how concerned he was, but he didn't like the sound of his aunt's cough or her pallid appearance. "How about I heat up a can of soup for you?"

She playfully swatted a hand at him. "I'll be fine, and later on when I'm hungry I can heat it up.

But thank you for the offer. Now you get on home to Mozart—I'm sure he's waiting on you. Besides, I don't want you catching my germs."

Reluctantly, he headed for the door, but then stopped and looked directly at his aunt. "I want you to promise me that you'll phone if you need anything at all. And if you're not better tomorrow, I'll drive you to the doctor." Not that he was scolding her, but Todd couldn't bear the thought of his aunt suffering if she just needed a prescription.

Ellen grinned and nodded. "I promise." More coughing followed.

After being certain she was okay, Todd left and drove to his apartment. Concern filled him as he thought about his aunt's appearance and how she'd sounded. If necessary, he'd phone his school and tell them to find someone to cover his classes, because he'd do whatever he could for her.

Sleep was difficult that night. He kept expecting the phone to ring, although it never did. When morning arrived, he was groggy as he dressed for work. Tempted to phone his aunt to check on her, Todd decided it would be best to wait. If she was sleeping and he woke her, he'd feel terrible.

His day with the students went smoothly, but during the last class of the day, his phone rang. He stepped to the classroom door to answer, not wanting to be within earshot of his students. When he heard his aunt's voice—sounding worse than the previous day—Todd's heart raced.

~ ~ ~

"Is it only Wednesday? Shouldn't today be Friday?" Zoey moaned to Meg at the entrance to the medical office that morning.

Meg grinned and patted her friend's arm. "You'll feel better after some coffee, Zoey. Maybe today won't be too crazy." Who was she kidding? Rare was a day of calm with all the patients they handled. But at least busy days made the time go quickly—not that Meg was wishing her life away—but she'd much prefer keeping busy than watching the clock.

Dr. Phipps whisked in the back entrance with a wave to his employees, then headed to his private office to prepare for the day. The aroma of brewing coffee drifted out of the small breakroom, and the workers scurried around as they accomplished their routine tasks.

As Meg perused that day's schedule, she saw it was pretty full. There were bound to be additional patients who phoned saying they needed to be seen right away. She stepped into the breakroom to pour her coffee and heard the receptionist already fielding incoming calls from patients.

Zoey entered the breakroom and sighed. "I'm already tired and we haven't even begun seeing patients yet." She shook her head and grabbed her coffee mug.

Before Meg had a chance to reply, the receptionist called her name. Olga needed help taking phone calls, so Meg rushed out to the office area. Oh yes, today would be hectic for certain. Between taking calls, greeting patients who entered the waiting room, and assisting the nurses as needed, the morning sped by.

When it was time for lunch, Meg was almost too tired to eat, but if she didn't, she'd feel weak and become shaky by mid-afternoon. So she nibbled at her salad and crackers, and indulged in a cola for more caffeine. Thankfully, the light lunch gave her a needed boost, and she was ready to complete the afternoon duties.

At three o'clock, she grabbed the appointment sheet and stepped to the doorway to summon the next patient. "Ellen Davis." Meg smiled at the elderly lady from her church. It was obvious the poor woman was ill—her nose was red, eyes watery, and she appeared weak—not at all the same person Meg had seen at church. "Hello, Miss Ellen. How are you?" How had the woman driven herself to the appointment in her weakened state?

Ellen offered a feeble smile. "I've had better days. Thank you for asking." Her voice was hoarse, as though it took effort to speak.

"I'm so sorry, but hopefully you'll be good as new very soon." Meg always tried to be upbeat with the patients, especially with elderly people. She escorted the patient to her room, where Zoey was ready to check her vital signs.

After returning to the main office area, Meg busied herself assisting the receptionist with phone calls and checking the incoming patient files. A male voice from the sign-in window startled her.

"Excuse me. I need to make sure my aunt got in okay." Todd smiled shyly at Meg. He appeared embarrassed for interrupting her, but after all, this was part of her job.

Meg stepped to the small window, and immediately caught a whiff of his cologne—a pleasing, woodsy scent. She smiled as she replied, "Hi, Todd. Yes, she's in an exam room with the nurse, and Dr. Phipps should be checking her soon."

Relief washed over his face. "Okay, thanks. I drove her here and made sure she got inside, but then needed to put gas in my car."

Meg nodded, then without giving it another thought, she questioned him. "Are you enjoying Coastal Breeze? I'm sure it's a bit different than Birmingham."

He nodded and grinned. "Yes, it sure is. But I like it here." He fidgeted, then headed to a chair and picked up a magazine from the nearby table.

Meg silently chided herself. She had work to do, so why was she making small-talk with Todd? *Because you'd like to know him better.* She didn't have time to dwell on that thought, because Olga called to her with a question about a patient. Meg needed to stay away from the sign-in window so she wouldn't be tempted to sneak glances at Todd. She went about her duties, but her mind traveled to the man in the waiting room.

About ten minutes later, the exam room door opened and Zoey escorted Ellen Davis to the check-out counter. As the elderly patient handed her credit card to the receptionist, she smiled at Meg. "I feel better since Dr. Phipps said I'm not dying." Her hoarse chuckle turned into a cough, and she shook her head. "I'm sure these prescriptions he gave me will do the trick."

Zoey grinned and gently patted the woman's

shoulder. "Yes, Ms. Davis, you'll feel much better soon. But if you need anything or have questions, please don't hesitate to call us, okay?"

The woman nodded as a sheepish look came over her wrinkled features. "I confess I wouldn't have phoned today if not for my wonderful nephew. Todd was so worried about me and insisted I call the doctor. He even left his job early so he could drive me. He's a jewel." Obvious pride shown on her face.

Zoey was needed in another patient's room, so she scurried away. Meg remained at the counter in case Ms. Davis had any questions. *Who am I fooling? I'm hoping for another glimpse of her jewel.*

Before Ellen took two steps into the waiting room, Todd was out of his seat and by her side. Concern shown in his gray eyes as he asked what the doctor had said, his gaze darting between his aunt and Meg.

Ellen flapped her hand as if swatting a fly. "I'll be fine. It's just a pesky respiratory infection, but I've got some good medicines to take." She grinned up at her nephew. "Will you have time to take me to the pharmacy, Toddles?"

Meg didn't miss the look of embarrassment at the nickname. He nodded at his aunt, but his face was beet-red.

"Take care, Miss Ellen, and if you need us just phone." Meg smiled and waved good-bye, then added an extra good-bye to Todd.

He sent her a quick smile before turning his full attention to his aunt. The pair slowly headed to his car.

Meg stepped back behind the counter to resume her duties. Zoey rushed up to her and gasped, "Your piano tuner is certainly attentive to his aunt. While I took her vital signs, she went on and on about her wonderful nephew. That's so sweet they have a close relationship." Zoey eyed Meg curiously, as if hoping for comments about him.

Trying to remain casual, Meg nodded. "Yes, that is sweet. He seems to be a doting nephew." She stopped talking about him before her perceptive friend was sure to figure out that Meg was more than a little attracted to him.

"Wow. Tall, good-looking, and thoughtful. What a great catch he'd be for someone." A teasing grin lit up Zoey's face and she giggled. But before Meg could respond, Dr. Phipps called to her with a question.

Whew. No way could Meg let her friend know just how appealing she found Todd Davis. But after seeing his concern for his aunt, that earned him more points in her mind.

~ ~ ~

Good grief. Why did Aunt Ellen have to call him by a pet name in front of Meg? What would she think of a man called by such a childish nickname?

Maybe she hadn't even heard his aunt. *Yeah, right.* Of course Meg would've heard Aunt Ellen, because she'd been standing only feet away from them at the time. Oh, well. What did it matter? And why did he keep thinking of her so often?

She'd told him she was widowed, but he figured she had someone in her life by now. Besides, she probably preferred a macho-type of man, which he wasn't. Sure, he was tall. But he'd always been on the slender side. Although he'd played soccer in his youth, he always preferred music and nature over sports.

Painful memories began to surface, as they did from time to time. His older cousin Earl's bullying ways when Todd was a child, then his ex-wife complaining that he wasn't into sports 'as most men were'—hurtful memories he tried to keep buried.

Driving to the elementary school the next morning, Todd told himself to stop fretting about the previous day's embarrassment, but instead be thankful his aunt wasn't gravely ill. Besides, he had bigger things to think about—his current job and what career path to take next. At least he could continue the piano tuning, but he couldn't make a living on that alone.

"Good morning, Todd." The receptionist greeted him warmly as the aroma of coffee reached his nose. The office was unusually calm for a school day, and a surprising realization hit him. In some ways, he would miss working here.

He hurried on to his classroom, hoping the young teacher who'd been extra-attentive to him didn't stop in his doorway to chat. As soon as he stepped to his desk, his cell phone rang.

"Toddles, you know I try not to bother you at work. But would you mind terribly picking up a can of chicken and rice soup for me on your way home after work? I do hate to trouble you, dear, because you've already done so much for your old aunt."

"Sure, Aunt Ellen. Do you need it before this afternoon? I'll leave school early if you do."

"Bless you. No, later this afternoon will be fine." Ellen cleared her throat before continuing. "You are wonderful. Some young lady will realize what a treasure you are and grab you up one day." A coughing spell erupted, so their conversation ended.

Before returning to his lesson plans, Todd replayed his aunt's comment. She really hoped he'd remarry someday, and he also knew she detested his ex-wife and the way she'd treated Todd.

Another thought formed in his mind right before the first class entered his room. If and when he ever remarried, he hoped his new wife would get along well with his aunt—someone who'd be kind and caring to Ellen. Without any bidding, the image of Meg formed in his mind. But he refused to linger on those thoughts, because lively first-graders rushed in eager to sing that day's songs.

~ ~ ~

As Meg drove home from work that afternoon, she blew out a sigh. Today had been as busy as the previous day, and she'd barely had time to nibble at a sandwich for lunch. *But today you didn't get to see your piano tuner and his sweet aunt.* Where had that thought come from?

Her musings were interrupted as her cell phone rang. Since she'd pulled into her driveway, she grabbed the phone and glanced at the caller ID. Ugh. Helena Mills was phoning her, and Meg was in no mood to listen to her late husband's stepmother. Yet if she didn't answer, the persistent woman would continue trying to reach her.

"Hello?" Meg attempted to keep her voice steady.

"Meg, it's Helena. I wanted to phone and see how you're doing." The forced niceness in her tone was more than a little obvious, causing Meg's stomach to tighten.

"I'm doing well, thank you." *And I'm positive you have another reason for phoning me. You're not interested in how I'm doing.*

Helena cleared her throat before speaking again. Meg steeled herself for whatever the woman was about to suggest. "Good. The other reason for my call is to see if you've reached a decision yet on the land that Roy owned. My attorney and I have been discussing it and are certainly willing to offer our help if you need it."

I'll bet you are. Meg tamped down the sarcastic words longing to escape her mouth. She absolutely would not be rude to Roy's stepmother, no matter how much the woman grated on her nerves. If Helena was even a tiny bit sincere, it might be different, but Meg knew her true motives and greedy nature.

Forcing a polite tone, Meg responded. "Thank you, Helena. I do appreciate your offers of help, but I'm still praying about what to do, and feel confident I'll make the right decision." Meg was more than ready to end this conversation.

To her relief the older woman simply told Meg she'd wanted to touch base with her, then said good-bye. While hurrying to her front door, Meg realized her hands were shaking. She didn't need to allow that woman to affect her in such a negative way.

She changed her clothes and fed her cats, then decided to head to the beach for a quick stroll. She'd eat supper after returning home, because there was no way she could eat anything at the moment.

"Be back soon." She spoke to Linus and Georgia, thankful for the felines' soothing presence in her life. The drive to her usual beach entrance took all of three minutes, and she pulled into the parking lot, relieved to have much of this stretch of beach to herself.

Minutes later she was walking barefoot along the shore, listening to the crashing waves of the high tide mingled with the squawk of hungry seagulls. She breathed in the April air, feeling refreshed simply by being close to the sea. Yes, moving to Coastal Breeze two years ago had definitely been the right thing for her to do after becoming widowed. Not to mention being much closer to her parents and much further away from Roy's stepmother.

Thoughts of Helena and her greedy intentions threatened to interrupt her pleasant walk, but Meg shoved away those bitter thoughts. Instead, she allowed her mind to imagine the business she hoped to start. Owning a small used-bookstore had been her dream for a long time, especially since Coastal

Breeze didn't have any shops devoted to books. A ripple of excitement ran through her, as it always did when she thought about her dream.

As she circled around to retrace her steps and head back to her car, Meg noticed an older couple strolling toward her, holding hands and laughing. She realized the woman was Ginny, the owner of the local gift shop. When they drew closer, Ginny stopped walking and grinned at Meg.

"Hello there, sugar. It's a lovely evening for a beach walk, isn't it?" Ginny used her free hand to smooth hair out of her face.

"Yes, ma'am, it sure is. I was just thinking that I'm so thankful I moved to Coastal Breeze two years ago."

Ginny's eyes widened. "Sweetie, have you met my husband, Claude Grover?" The older man smiled politely and shook Meg's hand. Whew, what a relief she'd not been digging in the sand for any shells.

"We haven't officially met, but I've seen him at church." Meg had often thought what a cute pair they were.

After a few more pleasantries were exchanged, they all continued on their way. Meg realized she was smiling as she thought about the couple, holding hands and acting like teens. Would she ever have someone to walk along the beach with while holding hands? Even if Roy had lived, Meg couldn't imagine him enjoying something like this.

Returning to her car, Meg brushed the sand off her feet and climbed inside. But for some unknown reason, the image of another man formed in her mind. A tall, shy man who was so unlike any guy that had appealed to her in the past. Why did her thoughts continue returning to him?

4

"I'm glad you're feeling better, Aunt Ellen." A wave of relief flowed over Todd after hearing his aunt's voice on Friday afternoon. A lingering trace of hoarseness remained, but overall she sounded more like her normal self. The prescriptions Dr. Phipps had given her were helping.

"Oh, you know what I always say. You can't keep a spry hen like me down for long." She laughed, but it soon turned into a coughing spell.

"Well, as happy as I am that you're doing better, I still want you to rest. I'm getting ready to leave the school parking lot, so why don't I pick up something you'd like at a restaurant?"

"You are an absolute angel. I won't refuse the attention from my favorite nephew." She cleared her throat before continuing. "I'll allow you to pick up something for supper only if you'll stay and eat with me. I promise I won't share my germs."

An hour later he joined his aunt in her cozy kitchen, the aroma of fried chicken wafting around them. Todd was secretly glad she'd requested fried chicken, because that was one of his favorite meals. He set everything on the table, and insisted Ellen not do a thing but take her seat.

"You're spoiling me, Toddles." She shook her head, but it was obvious she relished the attention. Surprisingly, her appetite was good, and she appeared to enjoy the meal. Since Todd had purchased extra servings, there were leftovers his aunt could enjoy the next day.

As Todd stood to clear the table and pour more iced tea in Ellen's glass, she gazed up at him with a seriousness. "Um, I hate to bring this up, but I recently had a phone call from Earl." She paused as if gauging his reaction.

Todd's gut tightened at the mention of his cousin. He remained silent, curious as to what his aunt would share. Not that he even wanted to think about the cousin he'd not seen in years.

Keeping her eyes focused on her glass of iced tea, Ellen spoke slowly, as if choosing her words carefully. "It was a brief conversation, and to be honest, I was surprised to hear from him. He sounded nervous, so I wondered if he was calling to ask for something."

Todd had a feeling his aunt was implying money, but she was too mannerly to say that. Ellen had always been a dignified, southern lady, and not one to speak harshly or be overly-critical of others—even about those who'd made bad choices. Earl was certainly in that category.

She continued, now meeting Todd's gaze. "He asked how I was doing, and I told him well. Then when I inquired about his well-being, he sounded down and out. He said he'd lost his job in Kentucky and was trying to decide what to do."

She lowered her eyes before continuing. "He asked how you were doing, and I told him well. But I didn't mention that you'd recently moved from Birmingham to Coastal Breeze. I figured if you want him to know, that information needs to come from you." She raised her eyes and offered a sympathetic smile.

Todd nodded, tamping down the mixture of emotions coursing through him. Drawing in a deep breath, he calmly questioned his aunt. "Did he ever mention his specific reason for calling you?"

Ellen shook her head and frowned. "No, but he did mention that he'd recently phoned several other relatives, so I can't help wondering if he's trying to get on good terms with the family again. Maybe show everyone that he's got his life straightened out." She lightly shrugged. "I don't know, but I certainly hope he's on the right path now. Anyway, I doubt he'll try to contact you, Todd, so no worries. Even if he did, you could keep the conversation brief. I know you and Earl weren't close."

Todd nodded at his aunt. "Maybe he is finally on the right path. We can only hope." *And I'm hoping he doesn't try to contact me. I have nothing to say to him.*

After reaching over and gently patting Todd's hand, Ellen brightened. "Now, how about some pie that dear Midge Weatherbee dropped off earlier? She said she was worried about me and knew I wouldn't feel like doing any baking, so she baked an apple pie and brought it to the front door." She released a hoarse-sounding giggle. "I think that's the briefest visit I've ever had with Midge. She's usually in no hurry to stop chatting. But I think she was afraid she might catch my germs."

Todd rose from the table to serve the pie, insisting his aunt remain seated. He was relieved she'd not lingered on the topic of his cousin Earl, because he most likely wouldn't be able to consume a single bite of pie.

Twenty minutes later, Todd gave his aunt a quick hug, reminding her to phone if she needed anything, and then drove to his apartment. He'd recently noticed that each time he returned to the small apartment, it made him more eager for a house. Nothing large, of course, but a more permanent residence than the minimal living space he and Mozart currently occupied.

Later that evening, Todd's thoughts threatened to return to his aunt's comments about Earl's phone call, but he shoved them aside. He didn't need to allow his mind to dwell there because thinking of Earl always dredged up horrible memories. Right now, Todd wanted to think about positive, uplifting things—such as finding another job and locating a home for himself and Mozart.

As if on cue, the feline brushed against his leg and gazed up at him. Todd leaned down to stroke the striped fur on the cat's back and spoke to his pet. "Yep, I need to focus on finding us somewhere else to live, Mozart. A house with more room, and more windows for you to birdwatch from."

The soothing purrs coming from the cat

seemed to affirm that he agreed with Todd, and minutes later while preparing for bed, Todd continued thinking about a new home. He'd start his house-search soon, complete his substitute teaching job, and get serious about finding another job. Lots of changes appeared to be on the horizon in his life, and that just might be a very good thing.

~ ~ ~

Saturday dawned sunny and warm with a light breeze—the perfect springtime day—so Meg needed to spend some time outdoors, and not only run errands. Since Zoey was supposed to have a date with Trevor, there would be no girlfriends' dinner out later that day. She might even indulge in picking up a meal, complete with French fries. After all, she hadn't treated herself to her favorite comfort food in a while.

When her cell phone rang, Meg's heart raced. What if Helena was phoning her yet again? Meg had nothing to say to her, and it wasn't as though they'd had a close relationship when Roy was living.

Why did she allow that woman to get to her? When Roy was living, he'd even made comments about his stepmother. After Roy's father had died, Helena's true personality came to light, and it had been apparent that she'd only been after money.

Meg knew what she planned to do about the property Roy had left her. She'd not only discussed the matter with her parents, but had prayed to make certain she was doing the right thing. Was Helena's interference actually coming from the enemy? A disconcerting thought, for sure. Meg's patience was wearing thin.

Lord, please help me handle this situation better. I need to be praying for Helena, because she's obviously not a happy person since she wants to control others.

The call had turned out to be a wrong number, but since the ringing of her phone had unsettled her, Meg knew it was time for some fresh air and exercise. She had the perfect place at her disposal, so she may as well take advantage of it.

Minutes later she was strolling along the wet sand, feeling the salty mist caressing her face. Turning her face toward the water, she was reminded of why this area was called the Emerald Coast. A beautiful name for a beautiful area. She breathed in the ocean air and paused to watch a couple of gulls determined to grab a fish. Pulling her gaze away from the blue-green water to look straight ahead, she noticed a tall man walking toward her. Yet he was further inland and not close to the water, almost as though he was keeping his distance from the ocean. *Todd.*

Her piano tuner was walking alone, and Meg's heart fluttered as she veered away from the water and headed closer to him. She attempted to smooth strands of hair from her face and flashed a smile up at him.

"Hello." Todd grinned shyly at her and stopped walking. He stood with his hands in his pockets, reminding Meg of a shy little boy, aside from his height, which was well over six feet.

"Hi there. It's great living at the coast, isn't it?" She was certain she must look a mess with her windblown hair.

His eyes darted toward the ocean, but quickly returned to Meg's face. "Yeah, I figured since I live so close to the beach, I might as well get some walking exercise here." His gaze now fixed on her.

Meg reached up to swipe hair out of her eyes. "Sometimes I still can't believe I do live so close to the ocean. But I'm glad I do." When he barely nodded, Meg assumed he wanted to continue with his walk.

"How's your piano doing?" Todd now had his arms hanging by his side, but quickly crossed them.

"It's wonderful, thank you. Your tuning made a huge difference, so now if I just practice enough, maybe my playing will be decent. And hopefully I won't frighten my cats." She laughed.

He grinned and nodded, his face even more appealing to Meg.

Her heart raced. How close they were standing, but Todd must have other things to do, so she reluctantly turned toward the water. "It's good to see you again. Have a nice afternoon."

Meg resisted the urge to turn around and watch him as he walked away. She headed back toward the water's edge and continued on with her walk.

As she picked up her pace, her thoughts remained on Todd. So far, her conversations with him had been somewhat limited, so she'd not been able to learn much about him. Maybe sometime she and Todd could walk together on the beach. Surely then he'd open up more. Wouldn't he? The silent question surprised her, but the image of walking beside him was appealing. *Very* appealing.

~ ~ ~

Encountering Meg on the beach that day had been an unexpected but nice surprise, yet also a bit awkward. How ridiculous he must've sounded asking about her piano. Good grief. *How's your piano doing?* Who talks like that? To Meg's credit she hadn't looked at him as though he was crazy.

He'd be more at ease the next time they spoke. After all, she was friendly and hadn't done anything to make him feel ill-at-ease. *Just my usual insecurities creeping in again.* Unfortunately, his ex-wife had only made them worse, with her almost-constant criticizing of Todd's shyness and love of music. She'd known she wasn't marrying an outgoing, athletic macho man, yet apparently Tara had thought she could change Todd once they were married.

Aunt Ellen's words echoed in his mind. Shortly after the divorce was final, Aunt Ellen had told him that no one should ever try to change him. She'd gone on to say that if he remarried, he needed to find someone who loved him the way he was. Another reason his aunt was so dear to him—she'd been there for him when his parents died, and then again when his marriage died.

His cell phone rang, and when he saw Ellen's number on the caller ID, he couldn't resist chuckling. "Hello, Aunt Ellen."

"Toddles, you sound very happy. Do you have

a friend visiting?"

He hurried to explain that he'd just been thinking about her wise advice after his divorce.

Now it was her turn to chuckle. "I'm not sure how wise I am, but thank you for letting me know that something I said encouraged you." After only a moment's pause, she continued. "The reason I'm phoning is to let you know that Pastor Jack wants to meet with you tomorrow. He said if you have time, right after church he'd like to speak with you for a few minutes."

Todd was puzzled. He'd met the pastor when his aunt had introduced them, but he couldn't imagine why the man wanted to speak with him. Possibly about joining a Sunday school class or a group for singles? But he learned the reason as Ellen continued.

"Pastor Jack has learned that you are musically talented. It so happens that our church is in need of a permanent choir director, so he's going to discuss the position with you. Isn't that wonderful?" Her voice rose with each sentence.

Todd had a sneaking suspicion as to how the pastor learned about his musical abilities. After thanking Ellen and assuring her that he'd pray about the job, Todd clicked off his phone. As he prepared for bed later that night, there was a ripple of excitement running through him at the thought of leading the choir. He'd wanted something music-related, and that job would certainly qualify.

At church the next morning, Todd had difficulty staying focused on the sermon, although the message was meaningful. His mind bounced between wondering what the pastor would say about the job, and watching Meg in the choir loft. Once, when their eyes met, she sent him a sweet smile, and a warmth covered his face.

When the service ended, Todd slowly filed out with the others, pausing as he shook the pastor's hand. "Todd, if you don't mind, hang around a little bit longer. After I finish speaking to folks, then we can step back inside the building to talk." The pastor eyed him kindly, and Todd nodded and thanked him.

Great. Now he'd stand awkwardly by himself as he waited for Pastor Jack. Ellen was chatting with several of her friends, so Todd avoided joining that group. But before he had another second to feel awkward, a female voice spoke his name.

Meg hurried toward him, grinning and clutching her handbag and a church bulletin. "So good to see you again. Since you'd asked about my piano yesterday, I wanted to let you know that you inspired me to sit down and practice last night." She laughed lightly and her blonde hair bounced gently on her shoulders. Her voice and laugh were so carefree. She shook her head. "I must be improving, because my cats actually sat in the living room while I played."

Todd beamed. "I'm glad to hear that your piano sounds better. And it's good you're practicing." Before he could add another sensible comment, the pastor joined the couple.

After Pastor Jack apologized for interrupting them, Meg assured him she was leaving. "See you later, Todd." She called over her shoulder as she headed to the church parking lot.

The men stepped into the worship building, and their meeting lasted all of ten minutes. Pastor Jack got right to the point, explaining that the temporary choir leader would be finishing in June, and the church needed a permanent replacement. He handed Todd a sheet with basic information, including the salary. Patting him on the shoulder, he told Todd to pray about the position, and if possible, give him an answer within two weeks. After shaking hands, the pastor locked the building.

Hurrying to his car, Todd's mind raced. This might be what he'd been praying for, but he would need to look over the information thoroughly and pray more about it. He had known that the salary wouldn't be much, but maybe combined with tuning jobs it would be sufficient. Besides, being the choir leader would be another opportunity to see Meg, and that just might make up for the small salary.

~ ~ ~

The following Friday afternoon, Meg headed to her bank on the outskirts of Coastal Breeze. As she waited in line for her turn, tiredness seemed to make each step an effort. It had been an unusually busy week at the medical office, and she hoped to catch her breath over the weekend.

While she waited for the bank teller, Meg's mind drifted to thoughts of starting her business. Would running her bookstore leave her this tired by the weekends? She still needed to work out her final plans. In all reality she'd need to be open on

Saturdays, too. Much to think about, but at the moment she wanted to finish her errands and return to her cottage.

Minutes later she exited the bank, feeling a bit revived as an ocean breeze swept through the parking lot. The late afternoon sunshine was warm, and Meg knew as summer approached the days would become even warmer. A movement to her left caught her eye.

An older woman hurried from a Mercedes toward the bank. Meg's breath caught in her throat. Was that Helena? Her pulse raced and her steps slowed.

The woman reached the bank's entrance, but apparently forgot something, because she whirled around and headed back toward her car.

With a big sigh of relief, Meg realized the woman was not her late husband's stepmother. And the woman didn't appear to have noticed Meg staring.

Silently chiding herself, Meg climbed into her car and sat for a couple of minutes. Was she becoming paranoid? Helena lived two hours away, so why would she possibly be at this bank anyway? *Spying on me.* The ridiculous thought flashed through Meg's mind. Helena's calls were affecting her too much.

She skipped going to the store and headed home. Maybe tomorrow she'd buy groceries, but if not, she had enough food for herself and her cats for another week. As soon as she was in her driveway and turned off her car, relief swept over her. Okay, she needed to get a grip on these feelings. Maybe a quick talk with Zoey would help.

Inside her cottage, Meg fed her cats, poured a glass of iced tea, and then phoned her friend. "Hey girlfriend, are you busy?" She almost felt silly phoning her since they'd been together at work all day, but she needed Zoey's perspective on this situation.

"No, just trying not to be perturbed with Trevor." Zoey emitted a teasing growl and then explained her boyfriend had cancelled their plans again. "He said his uncle needs help with some painting. Who paints on a Friday evening?" She blew out a long sigh.

A jab of guilt poked Meg. She'd phoned Zoey to be encouraged, yet her friend needed some encouragement herself. "I'm sorry, Zoey. At least Trevor is loyal to his family, which is a good sign. But that doesn't mean he should cancel plans with you unless it's an emergency. It's his loss." She hoped her paltry words would give her friend a lift.

Zoey laughed and thanked her. "I guess I shouldn't complain about Trevor so much, but you're always a good listener." After a slight pause, she continued. "Hey, are you okay? I didn't ask what you phoned me for? Anything wrong?"

"I feel silly for phoning you about this—especially after you have a legit reason to be upset right now." She drew in a breath before telling Zoey about seeing the woman in the bank parking lot. "For a few seconds, I actually thought that woman was Helena. Isn't that crazy?"

"No, it's not crazy, given everything that Roy told you about her. Plus, she's hounded you about the property Roy left to you."

Meg felt better after hearing her friend's words. It was true, because Roy had commented more than a few times that he hadn't trusted Helena. At the time, Meg had wondered if maybe Roy was resentful because his father had remarried, but after all the phone calls from the woman, it was evident that Roy had pegged his stepmother correctly.

~ ~ ~

Was he making a mistake? Todd's mind whirled with the information Pastor Jack had given him the previous Sunday. Maybe it would help him process everything if he saw it on paper. Locating a notebook from his desk, Todd nabbed a pen and sat at his kitchen table.

Ten minutes later he stared at the sheet of paper in front of him, filled with the basic information about being the choir director. To his surprise, a sizzle of excitement ran through him as he thought of this job. He loved music, so he could handle leading a church choir, right? After all, the pastor had assured him that the choir members were generally easy to work with. *But you're not a leader.* He ignored the nagging thought.

His mind switched gears to the financial aspect. Could he really make a decent living by being a choir director in addition to tuning pianos? Both were music-related, so that was in his favor. Still…doubts tugged at his mind.

The ring of his phone startled him. His aunt's name appeared on the caller ID. "Hello, Aunt

Ellen."

"Hello, Toddles, dear. Am I interrupting anything? I can phone later if I am."

He assured her that he wasn't doing anything important, then grabbed a bottled water from his refrigerator as he listened.

"I wanted to let you know that Earl phoned me again, and he wants to visit me soon. He asked about you—apparently one of our relatives had told him you relocated here from Birmingham." Ellen's normally confident voice held an underlying tone of uncertainty. "He said he'd like for the three of us to meet for dinner soon."

Todd's gut tightened and he gripped the phone. What was Earl up to now? There was no way his cousin simply wanted to reconnect with his relatives. No, he must have a motive. Maybe he was selling something and wanted Todd and his aunt to be customers.

"Are you there, Todd?"

Drawing in a deep breath, he kept an even tone. "Yes, ma'am, I'm here. Just surprised that Earl wants to visit after all these years." Truth be told, he had no desire whatsoever to see or talk to Earl—ever again. But he wouldn't express that to his kind-hearted aunt.

"Okay, you just let me know when Earl is planning to visit, and I'll make plans to be at your home to see him. Unless you'd rather not have him come to your house, Aunt Ellen. We could meet him at a restaurant—even one over in Destin."

"Yes, that's an idea. Maybe we'll do that."

"Please phone me if you need anything." Todd

hoped his aunt didn't hear his downcast tone. He'd need to mentally prepare himself before seeing Earl again.

Glancing down, Todd saw his cat sitting beside the food dish, looking up at him with that intent stare that only cats could have. "I guess I'd better feed Mozart. He's giving me that look."

Ellen lightly laughed and told him to give Mozart a hug from her, then the call ended.

As Todd opened a can of tuna for his beloved feline, his mind whirled with thoughts of his cousin trying to weasel back in their lives. That couldn't be a good thing—for any of them.

Yet he'd known that eventually he'd see his cousin again, and he only hoped that somehow Earl had changed—for the better. Todd couldn't handle those painful memories of his past being dredged up again. Especially not by the cousin who was the cause of the pain.

~ ~ ~

Meg's restlessness was increasing by the day, and that concerned her. She confided in Zoey as the two friends enjoyed dinner at The Happy Fisherman on Saturday.

"It's not that I don't enjoy my job, Zoey. Dr. Phipps and my co-workers are great." She released a long sigh. "It's just the fact that I'm over thirty now and I'm ready to move forward with my plans. I'm ready to start my business. My family is supportive, and they've encouraged me to do whatever I feel led to do, so that helps." She released a long sigh and reached for her glass of iced tea.

"So…what's the problem? Other than the fact you'd miss working with me." Zoey winked.

"I guess I'm afraid. It's a huge step, and there's so much to be considered. Not the least of which is the insurance coverage I'd need, but with the money I'd receive from selling Roy's property, I could manage." She hesitated and lowered her voice. "The man wanting to purchase the property is ready to buy, so it's just a matter of saying yes, I'll sell."

Zoey studied her. "Are you afraid that Cruella will cause problems if you go through with your plans? Remember, that woman has no voice in what you do with that property—or the money you'll make from selling it. Roy was your husband, and besides, Helena isn't even a true relative of Roy's."

Meg nodded. "You're right. But I'll admit it has crossed my mind more than once. Wondering if Helena would attempt to cause problems, although I have no idea what she could do other than keep phoning me and offering her 'advice,' as she calls it."

Their server appeared to see if they wanted dessert, which both women declined.

"I'd like a to-go box, please." Meg smiled up at the middle-aged waitress.

Zoey gestured to her empty plate. "As you can see, I don't need a box." The women laughed and the server left to get Meg's box.

"I'll eat my leftovers after church tomorrow. Are you doing something with Trevor?" Meg secretly hoped her friend had plans with the unreliable boyfriend.

Zoey shrugged. "Possibly. It depends how much work he and his dad accomplished today. I have to say, Meg, that you're better off with no boyfriend than one like I've got. Trevor can be a good guy when he wants to be, but he needs to mature. A lot." Zoey finished her last sips of tea.

Not wanting to add salt to Zoey's growing wound, Meg offered her friend a sympathetic smile. She couldn't agree more with Zoey's comments about Trevor, but stating that aloud would only make her friend feel worse.

"Oh, Meg…I'm so sorry. That didn't sound nice, did it? I shouldn't have made that comment about not having a boyfriend." Zoey's pitiful look of remorse reminded Meg of a puppy.

Meg giggled and squeezed her friend's hand. "No need to apologize. You were just speaking the truth."

"Okay, so tell me the plans for your bookstore." Zoey leaned closer on her elbows.

"Well, I've actually got a notebook filled with ideas." She began sharing some of her plans, pleased that Zoey appeared genuinely interested. The more Meg talked, the more she realized she needed to follow through with more than ideas. This was her dream, after all.

Twenty minutes later the women exited the restaurant, a lighthearted feeling sweeping through Meg, now accompanied by a breeze blowing in from the gulf. Heading to Zoey's car, the friends passed a family with several young children in tow.

After they climbed in the car, Zoey laughed.

"Those little kids we just passed could be your future customers. You mentioned having a section in your store devoted to books for children."

Meg shook her head at her friend, secretly pleased that Zoey had such confidence in her. "Thanks for being optimistic on my behalf. I'm only in the planning stages, and my best friend already has prospects for my business."

"Of course I do. What kind of a best friend would I be if I didn't encourage you?"

Although their comments were lighthearted, Meg appreciated Zoey's positive thinking. Her friend believed that Meg could achieve her dream.

Now if details fell into place and Helena stopped bugging her, the future would look bright. She'd still be single, but that was okay. If the Lord had someone for her, that would be wonderful. But if not, she would manage fine on her own. So why did the image of Todd Davis appear so frequently in her thoughts?

~ ~ ~

Todd had no desire at all to see his cousin Earl again. Not now, and not ever. Although a part of him actually felt sorry for Earl, the majority of his feelings toward the older cousin were not of pity, but of resentment. Along with some anger and a bit of fear.

He resented the way Earl had treated him when they were younger, mostly that horrible day at the lake. He didn't need to dredge up those painful memories. It served no purpose and always left him with a throbbing head or hurting stomach. Or both.

Ellen would let him know when they were to meet Earl, so until then Todd needed to keep his thoughts on finishing his present job and preparing to work at the church. Not to mention lining up more tuning appointments, too.

Swinging into his usual parking spot, Todd cut off his engine and headed into the building. The receptionist greeted him with a smile, then added that she hoped his students weren't acting wild.

Todd shook his head and smiled. "I can tell they're ready for summer break, but overall they're doing pretty well." He turned and strode down the hall to his classroom, relieved that he hadn't been stopped by anyone wanting to visit. Of course, by now the other teachers had likely figured out that the substitute music teacher was an introvert.

That thought brought to mind someone who was definitely *not* an introvert—at least from all appearances. Meg seemed the type of person who was always outgoing and friendly. So why did he feel a pull toward her? After all, his ex-wife had been an extrovert and that marriage had failed. Would that happen again? Todd knew he must guard his heart—there was no way he could endure another failed marriage.

Later that day, Todd was preparing to leave his classroom when his cell phone rang, showing his aunt's name on the ID. "Hi, Aunt Ellen. Do you need something from the store?"

"Hello, Toddles. No, thank you for asking, though. I wanted to let you know that Earl phoned me again today and he wants to visit with us this

Saturday. Does that work for you? I wasn't sure if you'd have a piano tuning appointment."

Todd's gut felt as though it had been punched, and he was thankful he wasn't driving home yet. He'd have trouble focusing on his drive during this conversation. "No, I don't have an appointment, so Saturday is fine." What else could he say? His aunt wasn't any more eager to see Earl than he was, but she was making the effort.

"I know this isn't something either of us look forward to, but I feel we should at least meet with him for a little while. How about lunch at The Happy Fisherman? I'll treat you both."

"That's kind, Aunt Ellen, but you don't need to treat. Yes, that restaurant sounds fine. I'll drive, so whatever time you want to meet is good." After his aunt decided on noon and assured Todd that she'd phone Earl with the details, their call ended. Before leaving his classroom, Todd sat at the desk for a few more minutes, digesting the call with his aunt. He had nothing to say to the older cousin who'd tormented him in their youth. No doubt he needed to pray before seeing Earl again.

That evening as he heated up a microwave meal and fed Mozart, Todd lifted up a quick prayer. As a Christian, he couldn't control his cousin's words or actions, but he could display a loving attitude toward the man. Whatever reason Earl had for making an appearance again would have to be handled carefully. Regardless of whether or not the man had changed was not Todd's concern. He needed to respond to his cousin as a Christian, and something told him it would be a challenge.

~ ~ ~

"Maybe we'll beat the large weekend crowd at the restaurant." Meg commented as Zoey drove the two of them to The Happy Fisherman on Saturday a little before noon. "It was pretty busy last Saturday, but we arrived later."

"I sure hope so, and that means we'll get our meal quicker. I didn't eat any breakfast so I'm starving." Zoey pulled into a parking spot not far from the door.

Minutes later the friends were seated and sipping glasses of sweet iced tea. "Okay, so tell me what's going on with Trevor." Meg eyed her friend and hoped she wasn't about to share some disheartening news.

Zoey took another swig of tea and then set her glass down with emphasis, nearly spilling some of the liquid. "Oh, he's just being Trevor, and I should be used to his lack of dependability by now. But I'm not. He'd talked like we had a date this weekend, then phoned yesterday to say he needed to help his dad again." She shook her head. "By the way, thanks for joining me today on such short notice. You're a true friend."

Meg offered a sympathetic smile. "I'm always happy to join you. Besides, it's not as if I have a full social calendar." Her comment brought a smile from Zoey.

Their server came to take their food orders, and as soon as she walked away, more customers entered the restaurant. Meg was about to lift her glass for another sip of tea, but stopped midway to her lips. The three adults who were being seated caught her attention. Todd, his aunt Ellen, and a man she didn't recognize took their seats at a table on the opposite side of the restaurant.

"Who do you see?" Zoey stared curiously at her, turning her head in the direction her friend was gazing.

"The three people who just came in. It's Todd and his aunt. But there's a man with them who looks…" Her voice trailed off as she tried to find the right words. "Well, he doesn't look like someone Todd would hang out with—not that I've met any of his friends." Her face heated up.

Zoey, being her usual perceptive self, arched an eyebrow and supplied a description. "Rough and seedy?"

"Yes, that pretty much describes his appearance. Definitely not Todd's type, from what we've seen of him so far." She tried not to stare, but couldn't quell her curiosity at the contrast between Todd and the man. His unkempt hair and numerous tattoos contrasted with Todd's neat appearance. Although Todd's hair often appeared a bit shaggy, his overall appearance was clean.

"I know it's wrong to judge by appearances. I shouldn't have even speculated about that man's character, because I know nothing about him."

Zoey gave her an understanding smile. "Hey, you're not the only one. I would guess that he's likely a rowdy type of guy." Zoey offered a smile before gesturing that their server was approaching with their meals.

Meg offered a quick blessing for their food, and silently asked forgiveness for her comments about the stranger at Todd's table. She'd have to focus on her conversation with Zoey and not wonder about the mystery man. *Or sneak glances at Todd.*

"Mmm…this shrimp is so good." Zoey's eyes closed for a second as she savored her meal.

"Yes, my flounder is delicious, and so are the hushpuppies." Meg tried to keep her eyes from straying to Todd's table, but the small group didn't appear to be meeting for a social visit. In fact, Ellen was doing the talking as the two men sat silently, looking rather glum. How odd.

As if reading her thoughts, Zoey grinned between bites. "Are you still trying to figure out the rough character with your piano man?"

Meg almost choked as she heard her friend's question. "My piano man? He's my piano tuner, but I wouldn't call him *my man*." She wasn't fooling Zoey. It occurred to her she'd genuinely like for Todd Davis to be *her* man. And that thought in itself was enough to cause her to choke again.

Zoey's eyes widened. "You know, he's really a good-looking guy, shaggy hair and all. I think the two of you would be a cute couple."

"Thank you for your compliment, but he has no interest in me." She popped a bite of potato in her mouth as she tried to think of a way to change the topic without being too obvious.

To her relief, Zoey received a text from her mother about returning home from the mission field, so the topic was switched without Meg's help.

She asked her friend some questions, which Zoey eagerly answered as the women continued their meal. Although Zoey missed her parents, she was proud of their work in Africa.

The women remained seated after their lunch, although Todd and his group had left. With the positioning of the tables, neither he nor his aunt had noticed Meg, which was a relief. She would've been embarrassed if they saw her staring at the man with them.

She spent the remainder of her afternoon with Zoey. The women stopped by Ginny's gift shop, then headed to Meg's cottage for coffee and more conversation.

Later that day as she waved good-bye to her friend, Meg thought about Todd yet again. Who was that man with them at the restaurant?

But even more than wondering about the mystery man, Meg couldn't stop thinking about Zoey's comment. *The two of you would be a cute couple.* She couldn't deny that the thought of Todd being in her life was very pleasing, but was that even a possibility?

5

Saturday night Todd reached for stomach medicine in his cabinet, thankful he kept antacids on hand. When his divorce had been fresh, he'd often had to take one of the tablets to soothe the pain from his clenched gut. Fortunately, as time went on, the pains had lessened and rarely ever occurred—until now. The lunch earlier that day with his aunt and cousin Earl had definitely been stressful. Of course, the fried seafood on his plate didn't help his digestion either.

He sat at his piano and played a few of his favorite tunes, attempting to block out thoughts of lunch. Not that anything dramatic happened, but still—just seeing Earl again caused tension in his gut. If only Todd could permanently block out all the taunts from childhood, not to mention that traumatic day at the lake.

Todd's fingers stilled on the piano keys as he fought the painful memories. At that moment a text came through on his phone. A message from his good friend, Chip Ledbetter, gave him an escape from his thoughts. His buddy in Birmingham wanted to talk the next day. Todd replied saying he'd phone him in the afternoon.

He'd missed hanging out with Chip and would welcome a phone conversation with him. Although married with a toddler, he still made efforts to keep in touch with Todd.

The next morning at church, Todd greeted his aunt and noticed she was eyeing him closely. She leaned over to him, her voice barely above a whisper. "Toddles, are you okay, dear? I hope our lunch yesterday didn't bring back too many difficult memories for you."

Bless her heart—Aunt Ellen was always concerned about him. Todd shook his head and managed a smile. "No, I'm fine, but thank you for asking. It did feel a bit strange seeing him again, but hopefully he was sincere and has changed for the better." Although after seeing Earl at the restaurant, Todd had his doubts. The haggard appearance of his cousin made him seem much more than six years older than Todd.

Throughout the worship service, Todd had to push away all thoughts of Earl and stay focused on the pastor's sermon, which was excellent as usual. He also tried not to think of taking over as choir director in another month, because that thought was enough to make his gut clench again.

When the service ended, Todd hugged his aunt good-bye and headed toward the doors to leave. When he reached them, somebody called his name. Turning around, he saw a smiling Meg coming toward him. His pulse sped up.

"I just wanted to say hello and ask how your substitute teaching job is going."

Todd glanced at the floor before meeting her gaze again. Why did this woman affect him this way? He offered a smiling nod. "It's going well, thanks." He grasped the paper bulletin in his fingers, hoping his hands weren't shaking.

Meg spoke again. "I saw you in The Happy Fisherman restaurant yesterday, but knew you didn't see me. My friend and I were seated on the other side. Did you have a good lunch?"

He nodded, surprised that she'd seen him, realizing that meant she'd also seen Earl. *Great.* "Yes, my meal was delicious. My aunt says that's her favorite restaurant."

This small-talk was becoming more awkward by the second. Why couldn't he think of anything brilliant or catchy to say?

As if reading his mind, Meg grinned and gestured toward the door. "Guess I'd better get moving. I'm supposed to visit my family this afternoon, and I never know how traffic is going to be on the route I take. See you later, Todd." Her gaze held his for a few seconds as he nodded.

Todd couldn't pull his eyes away as she walked to her car. Nor could he dismiss the thought that he'd like to get to know her better. He wasn't sure what it was, exactly, but there was something special about Meg Mills. Something that drew him to her, introvert though he was.

Todd shook his head. He needed to stay focused on his job situation and securing more clients for his tuning business. But it might be a good idea to pray about his friendship with Meg. After all, sometimes friendships grew into more. Much more.

~ ~ ~

"What's going on, girlfriend?" Zoey's voice held concern as she eyed Meg at work on Monday morning.

Meg shrugged, knowing she needed more coffee before tackling the busy day ahead. "Oh, it's Helena. She phoned me again last night and as a result, I didn't sleep well." Meg felt pathetic admitting that, although it was true.

In true Zoey fashion, her friend bristled and emitted a low growl. "Again? Why doesn't that woman realize you don't want to talk with her? Did she pester you about Roy's property again?" Zoey finished her coffee in a gulp, then dabbed her mouth with a napkin.

Thankfully no one else was in the employee breakroom at that moment. Meg didn't want any co-workers other than Zoey knowing about her former mother-in-law—or rather, stepmother-in-law. Roy would be shaking his head in disgust if he knew what the older woman was up to, and Meg was starting to feel pretty disgusted herself, simply thinking of Helena Mills.

"Yeah, just her same old tactics. Playing the concerned stepmother, she called to see how I was getting along, then she segued into talking about my inheritance, and her so-called advice for me."

Zoey placed a hand on Meg's shoulder, her

tone stern. "Ignore her calls. You don't need to deal with her, and you shouldn't have to. Doesn't she have anything else to do?"

Meg again shrugged and finished her last sip of coffee, but before the women could discuss the matter further, Olga called to them. They both scurried from the breakroom into the main office area.

The receptionist flashed a look of concern. "Just wanted you to know that Dr. Phipps has to attend the funeral of a relative tomorrow, so we'll need to double-up on his appointments to get everyone worked in. Hopefully the patients affected by this will be cooperative, but we never know how some folks will react. So, be warned, just in case." She blew out a sigh and grabbed the ringing phone.

"Never a dull moment." Meg forced a smile as she and Zoey got busy.

The hectic day was actually a blessing, Meg later realized. At least she wasn't able to fret about Helena's most recent phone call. A sliver of guilt poked at her. *If I prayed about the situation enough, then I'd never need to fret about Helena or anything she says.*

At home that evening, Meg finished feeding her cats when her phone rang. Zoey's concerned voice came through. "I wanted to check on you. You seemed really preoccupied today, even though we were crazy-busy."

God bless Zoey. She was a true friend, and Meg was thankful to have her in her life. Forcing out a light laugh, Meg attempted to sound like herself. "I'm fine, but you're sweet to be concerned.

It's just the usual Helena situation. Maybe her intentions are sincere, but I've let her know that I've reached a decision about selling the land. She refuses to accept—or believe—it."

Zoey released a sarcastic snort. "Good intentions? Helena? I don't think so. You're being too kind about that woman, Meg. Why do you think I refer to her as 'Cruella' anyway? It's because the woman has an evil side—you know she does."

Meg sighed. She couldn't argue, because she knew Zoey was right. Roy had even told Meg that he knew Helena expected all his father's inheritance, but instead, Roy had received most of it. Then after Roy's passing, the money and the property had gone to Meg.

"You're right, Zoey. It's sad, but true. It's just that her offers to advise me have caused me to doubt my goal of starting my own business." Before she could continue, her friend jumped in, her voice louder this time.

"Girl, listen to you. You were Roy's wife and the rightful owner of that piece of land, along with the funds he left to you. It's your land and money to do with as you please. Period. No matter what his stepmother or anyone else thinks, it's *your* decision." Zoey hesitated a moment before asking. "Have you talked to your family about this?"

"Yes, and they support whatever I want to do. They realize I've had a dream of owning and running my own used bookstore for years. Even when Roy was alive, he knew that's what I wanted to do someday." Her voice caught in her throat as a wave of sadness washed over her. Although her marriage to Roy had many strife-filled moments, Meg was still saddened at the early demise of her husband.

"Okay, then. Everyone who cares about you knows about your goal, and we all want you to achieve this. So whatever Cruella—I mean Helena—advises is a moot point. Focus on what *you* want to do, Meg."

Hearing Zoey's words gave Meg the boost she needed. How much lighter her spirit felt already. "Thanks, Zoey. I don't know what I'd do without you." The conversation switched to the hectic times at work that day, and they were both giggling before the call ended.

When Meg clicked off her phone ten minutes later, she knew she must focus on moving forward with her plans. If Helena continued phoning to offer input, then Meg would politely but firmly remind her that she'd decided what to do. She'd be kind to Helena, but there was no way she'd let the woman control her future.

~ ~ ~

When Todd arrived at his aunt's house on Thursday, she appeared and sounded more like her normal self. She appeared to be on the mend from her sickness and assured him she'd be completely well soon.

"I hope your hamburger is good. I ordered it with cheese."

"Mmm. I know it will be delicious, Toddles. You're so sweet to pick up supper and eat with me.

I'm afraid I've been overdoing it the past two weeks, since I thought I was getting well." Ellen laughed before a coughing spell flared up.

"I was happy to pick up supper, and as I've told you before, I never mind running errands for you or bringing food. I could never repay all you've done for me." His words were sincere, because she truly had been like a second mother to him.

At that moment her phone rang. Ellen grabbed it from the kitchen counter.

It didn't take long for Todd to figure out who'd phoned her. *Earl.* His aunt's guarded tone and wary expression were the only clues he needed. Why was his cousin coming back in their lives now? Did he have an ulterior motive—making thinking he could get some of Ellen's money?

Her conversation with Earl was brief, and to Todd's relief she'd not mentioned that he was there. Her face had grown paler while listening to her nephew, then the call ended after three minutes.

Aunt Ellen returned to her seat at the kitchen table and blew out a sigh. "That young man is something else." She appeared to be collecting her thoughts, so Todd remained silent as he nibbled a French fry.

"Earl was phoning to ask if I had any odd jobs he could do while he's in the area. He mentioned that he was running low on money and needed to pick up some cash while he was out of work." She shook her head and frowned. "I know he's family, but I'm not about to hand money over to him so he can squander it away."

Todd nodded his agreement. "You did the right

thing." He had a strong suspicion that Earl was trying to play on his aunt's sympathies. "At our lunch the other day he'd mentioned staying in a cheap motel and doing odd jobs for the owner. If the owner has nothing else for him to do, Earl needs to head home to Kentucky."

"I agree. Of course, he did say that his car needs some work, so maybe he's hesitant to drive it until it's repaired. He didn't say exactly what's wrong with his car, but I don't think he's been able to drive it since arriving in our area." Ellen released a worried sigh and shook her head. Her brow was creased. "I hope he wasn't expecting me to offer him a room here. I just don't think I'd be comfortable with him under my roof."

Todd's pulse raced. "No way does he need to stay here. You don't owe him a thing, and especially since you had no idea he'd be visiting this area. We still aren't even sure why he made the trip down here." Although Todd was relatively certain it was in hopes of getting money from Ellen.

His aunt flashed him a smile. "Thank you, Toddles. I want to do the right thing, but given Earl's background, I feel I must be careful." She rose from the table to pour them each a glass of iced tea. "Now, tell me about your substitute teaching job. I hope those students aren't giving you trouble."

The remainder of the visit held no more mention of Earl. During Todd's drive home, he couldn't help thinking about his cousin's reappearance in their lives. Just as a dark cloud hovered over the beach threatening a storm, Earl's presence had caused an uneasiness for Todd, and he hoped the man wouldn't cause any storms within their family. Especially not for his aunt.

~ ~ ~

It was time to move forward with her dream. Meg kept telling herself that each morning as she drove to her office manager job for Dr. Phipps. Yet each day's busy activities in the office kept her from actually doing anything towards her dream. By the time she left work in the afternoon, she was on the verge of exhaustion.

As she drove home on Friday afternoon, she realized yet another week had zipped by and she wasn't one step closer to achieving her goal of having a used bookstore. On a positive note, at least Helena hadn't phoned her this week. A blessing not to be taken lately.

After feeding her cats and preparing a sandwich for her supper, a restlessness filled her. When she finished eating, she phoned her parents to see if her dad could accompany her to meet with the loan officer at the bank.

"Glad to go with you, Meg. Just tell me when. Since I'm retired, it's not a problem. Besides, your mom will be happy to know I'm doing something productive—although I keep telling her my golf games are productive." He laughed, and hearing his laughter reminded Meg of how blessed she was to have healthy parents who were a part of her life. Although they were overbearing at times, they wanted what was best for her.

Zoey squealed into the phone the next morning when Meg told her.

"Yay! And you are so lucky to have your dad going with you. I think it helps in certain situations when an older adult is involved. Not that your dad is elderly or anything." Zoey giggled.

Meg couldn't help laughing. "I know what you mean, and I agree with you. Which is another reason I asked Dad to go with me. Besides, I'll be so nervous that the bank employees will wonder if I've just robbed another bank or something."

"We need to celebrate because you're finally moving forward with your dream. And just think—when you actually open your bookstore, we'll throw a huge party." Meg was touched by the excitement in her friend's voice. What a blessing Zoey was in her life.

The friends decided to order pizza and eat at Meg's cottage. After the call ended, Meg got busy with her usual Saturday tasks, but now filled with anticipation about finally realizing her dream. As she did laundry, vacuumed, and got ready for Zoey to join her for supper, her spirits soared.

"Look at you, grinning like the Cheshire Cat." Zoey teased her when she arrived.

"Your enthusiasm gave me a boost. You're such an encouragement. You helped me realize I can do this." Meg wanted Zoey to realize how much her words and attitude had helped.

"Hey, what are friends for? Heaven knows you've listened to me moan and groan about Trevor ad nauseum." Both women laughed, and then the talk turned to pizza choices.

While waiting for their pizza to be delivered, the women continued visiting, when suddenly Zoey's eyes widened. "I almost forgot to tell you—this morning I was in the grocery store and caught a glimpse of a really tall guy. For a second, I thought it was your piano man. But when I got a closer look, it wasn't him. In fact, whoever this guy was, he wasn't nearly as cute as your guy." Zoey giggled.

Meg knew her face was turning cherry-red, but she attempted a casual eye-roll. "I don't know why you refer to him as 'my guy,' Zoey. I still hardly know him." She didn't add that she'd like to know him better. Yet why was she hiding her feelings from Zoey? Her best friend knew her well.

More than ready to change the subject, Meg pulled out her notebook filled with plans for her bookstore. Yes, it was an obvious change of topic, but it worked. To her relief, Zoey didn't mention Todd again that evening.

But later that night, as Meg prepared her clothes for church the next morning, she couldn't deny hoping that a certain piano tuner would be there. And maybe she'd get to visit with him a bit. After all, he seemed like a nice guy, and it wouldn't hurt to be friendly, would it?

~ ~ ~

"I invited Earl to attend church this morning, but I haven't seen him." Ellen glanced around the worship building and then shook her head. "I hate to say it, Todd, but I had a feeling he wouldn't show." She blew out a sigh.

Todd had sympathy for his aunt yet also relief for himself. If Earl had shown up in church, he'd be sitting with them, which would mean when the service ended there would be conversation. Most likely Ellen would end up inviting Earl to join her for lunch, insisting that Todd come along, too.

Guilt poked at him. Here he was, sitting in church and feeling relieved that his wayward cousin hadn't shown up. Shame. Yet, given the background he had with Earl, he honestly had no desire to be around the man. The lunch at The Happy Fisherman had been uncomfortable enough.

Still, he couldn't help feeling pity for his aunt. "I'm sorry, Aunt Ellen. You invited him, which was very kind. You can't control what he does or doesn't do."

The older woman offered him a sweet smile, then patted his arm. "Thank you, dear. What a shame Earl didn't turn out to be like you."

At that moment the piano music began, so their conversation ceased. Todd watched the choir during the opening hymn, trying to imagine himself leading the group. A mixture of excitement and fear ran through him. Would the group be easy to lead? Would he feel flustered since Meg was a choir member? He again noticed her exuberance as she sang with the group. It was obvious her heart was in the music. *A fellow music-lover. A most-important trait you share.*

When the service ended, Todd told his aunt he'd see her later. She'd want to visit with her friends as she always did after church, so he made his way to the door.

Just as he stepped outside, a female voice reached his ears. Meg. He recognized her sweet, southern drawl right away, and his pulse raced. Why on earth did she affect him this way?

"Hi, Todd. How are you?" She stepped closer to him, emanating a fresh, floral scent. Her blonde hair hung loosely on her shoulders, and the coral-colored dress she wore brought out her blue eyes.

He grinned shyly at her. "I'm fine, how about you?"

A high-pitched laugh escaped her pink lips, and she blushed. "I'm okay. Just a bit nervous about a new business venture I'm embarking on." She reached up and smoothed some stray hairs away from her face.

"Oh? Are you starting your own business?" With her outgoing personality, he assumed she'd be successful at most anything she decided to do.

After a hesitant nod, she leaned toward him and spoke in a lowered voice. "Yes, Lord willing I'll be opening a used bookstore in the not-too-distant future." Another nervous laugh followed her words.

"Congratulations. I hope it goes well for you." Good grief. Could he sound any more stiff and formal? He fidgeted with his bulletin.

"Thanks, Todd. Not many people know about this, and I've only recently mentioned it to my boss, Dr. Phipps. Since I have no idea when I'll actually be ready to open my store, it looks like I'll be working for the doctor a while longer."

Good. That meant if Todd accompanied his aunt to the doctor, he'd likely see Meg there as he'd done before. Yet if he couldn't be more relaxed with her, then what was the point?

He nodded and smiled. "I'm sure Dr. Phipps will be sorry to lose a good employee."

She scrunched up her nose in a cute way, giggling as she responded to his compliment. "I don't know about that. But he said he will, so that makes me feel good, at least." She blew out a sigh. "There's just so much to do, even though my shop will be small. I've been collecting used books for years, so just getting them unpacked and arranged in the bookstore will be a job."

Without giving it a second thought, Todd said, "I'd be glad to help you unpack books." As soon as the words left his mouth, he saw her surprised look and blushed.

"Really? That'd be great, if you don't mind." She flashed a radiant smile at him, and Todd gripped his bulletin so tightly it was a wonder it didn't tear in half.

"Sure. I'm finishing a substitute teaching job, and have a few piano tuning appointments lined up, but other than that, I'm free." *Because I basically have no social life.*

The warmth in Meg's eyes sent his heart into overdrive—he'd only offered to help unpack books, yet the look she sent made it appear he'd offered her a lavish gift.

"I really, really appreciate your offer to help. What's the best way to contact you?"

"You can phone or text me." With shaking hands, Todd managed to lift his phone from the pocket of his pants.

The pair exchanged cell numbers, then Meg thanked him again.

"I'm heading to see my parents this afternoon, so I'd better run. You have a nice afternoon. See you later." She sent another sweet smile before heading to her car, drawing Todd's attention to those pink lips again.

He couldn't help wondering what it might be like to kiss those lips. And run his fingers through her thick, blonde hair, which appeared golden in the bright sunshine. *Snap out of it and quit staring. You're not in middle school.* A quick glance around let him know that no one had noticed him, standing there mesmerized by Meg Mills. He hurried on to his car.

That whole afternoon he couldn't stop thinking about Meg, and he realized he was actually looking forward to helping unpack books. At least that was an opportunity to be with her.

No doubt about it—Meg would be a great catch for some lucky guy. But not for someone like Todd, who was shy and had a failed marriage behind him.

Yet Meg had gone out of her way to speak to him more than once. Was she simply being friendly, or could there be an attraction there on her part? He was likely fooling himself, but the thought that Meg might feel drawn to him gave his heart a boost. A much-needed boost.

~ ~ ~

The following Wednesday afternoon, Meg drove home from her appointment at the bank, which was located not far from her parents' home. The meeting with the loan officer had gone well, and the added security of having her father present had calmed her nerves. Since Meg's parents were long-time customers at the bank, her dad had been greeted warmly when they entered the building.

Meg was overwhelmed as her mind whirled with all the information she'd received. Her heart raced to think that her dream would finally be coming true. Yet there was still much to be done, including numerous details to work out, not the least of which was being able to rent the desired building space in Coastal Breeze. That would be her next big step.

After entering her cottage, she fed her cats and changed clothes. She craved a walk on the beach—maybe that would calm her and help sort out all the information bouncing around in her head.

Since it was almost six o'clock, Meg hoped the beach wouldn't be crowded since many folks ate supper at that time. Sure enough, only a handful of beachgoers strolled along the sand, as the April wind blew in from the gulf and the seagulls coasted above the water. Meg never tired of this view and continued being thankful she'd made the decision to relocate to Coastal Breeze after becoming widowed.

Stepping along the wet sand at the water's edge, she felt refreshed. Her concerns about meeting with the loan officer and her busy day at Dr. Phipps's office seemed to drift away in the wind. She breathed in the salty air, allowing her mind to clear. It was amazing how a few minutes on the beach could have such a soothing effect. When she returned to her car fifteen minutes later, she noticed two missed calls—both from Helena. Her calmness evaporated as she stared at her phone screen. Why was Roy's stepmother phoning her again?

Pulling into the driveway at her cottage, Meg realized she was gripping the steering wheel. Had the walk on the beach been for nothing? She wouldn't let Helena Mills cause such stress in her life. Except that was exactly what was happening, and it needed to stop.

Inside her cottage, she lingered at the kitchen table before deciding to return Helena's call. Attempting to maintain a calm, even tone, Meg spoke after the woman answered.

"Hi, Helena. I saw I'd missed a call from you." Okay, actually two calls, but Meg wouldn't mention that.

"Yes, I phoned earlier to see how you're doing." Helena's voice was thick and her words slurred. What was going on?

"I'm fine, thank you. I was taking a walk on the beach so that's why I wasn't available to answer your call." Not that Meg owed her an explanation.

Helena's voice increased in volume. "Oh, how lovely." She paused, and the distinct sound of ice rattling in a glass came through the phone. From the way her voice sounded, the glass didn't hold cola or tea.

Meg was about to ask if she was okay, but before she could, the woman spoke again—this time even louder with more slurring of her speech.

"Tell me, Meg…have you decided what to do

with the property poor Roy left to you?" More clinking of ice cubes sounded in the background.

Fighting the urge to shut off her phone, Meg released a sigh. "Yes, Helena. I've handled that matter, but I appreciate your concern. I'm sorry, but I really need to go now. Good-bye." With that, she clicked off her phone and placed it on the table.

Her hands were shaking so badly that she didn't think she could pour herself a glass of tea. *Calm down. I did the right thing.* She opened her refrigerator and lifted out a pitcher of tea. Surprisingly she didn't spill any as she poured.

Meg's stomach rumbled, reminding her she hadn't eaten supper. Hopefully she could get down a bowl of soup and a few crackers. Minutes later, she sat at her table taking tiny bites of the vegetable soup. Her ringing cell phone startled her, and she dropped her spoon into the bowl with a clatter. Surely Helena wasn't calling her again, because Meg had nothing left to say to her.

Almost afraid to answer, Meg glanced at the caller ID. Seeing Zoey's number was a huge relief, and she answered in a wobbly voice.

"Meg? Are you okay? You sound…different." Zoey knew her well.

She managed a reply. "Yeah, I'm okay. Let's just say I'm glad it's you calling me."

"Oh no…did Cruella phone you again?" Zoey's tone held exasperation. "You need to ignore her calls."

"Yes, unfortunately she did. And it was her usual question about my decision on the property Roy left to me. But this time it was obvious she'd been drinking." Meg paused, giving Zoey a chance to absorb that information.

"What? Good grief, she's a mess." Zoey blew out a sigh before continuing. "Meg, you don't need that crazy woman bugging you. And the fact you could tell she'd been drinking when she phoned shows she must have some real issues. Of course, we've known all along she's nuts. I'm sorry, but that's the truth."

Despite the frustrating topic of their conversation, Meg released a giggle. "Thanks. You're the best. I feel better already."

"Hey, what are friends for? If I were a bit more assertive, I'd find Cruella and have a face-to-face talk with her and tell her to leave you alone."

"I don't think that would be wise, because no telling what she's likely to do. Seriously, now that I'm aware she might be a heavy drinker, she could be one of those people who turns violent under the effects of alcohol." Although Zoey had been joking about talking to the woman, Helena had major issues. She'd never want Zoey or herself to be at risk by confronting her—no matter how much she annoyed Meg.

Ready to change the topic, Meg asked about Trevor. "Any updates in the romance department?"

Zoey sighed. "Not really. And the clock is ticking. I'm ready to give him an ultimatum, because I'm not getting any younger."

Meg chose her words carefully. "Zoey, I know you really care about Trevor and he seems like a nice guy, but you don't deserve to be strung along. Maybe you should ask him where you stand."

"You're right. I know he's hesitant since his older brother went through a divorce. But that doesn't mean the same thing will happen to Trevor." Zoey paused. "Speaking of romance, have you seen your piano tuner recently?"

Meg was thankful she and her friend were talking on the phone rather than face-to-face. Why did the mere mention of Todd send a warm blush creeping up her face? She forced a casual tone. "Only at church. When I told him about starting a used bookstore, he offered to help me unpack boxes."

Zoey giggled. "You two would make such a cute couple. And the way you look at each other—I can tell there's something there. Maybe when he helps you, then you'll get to know each other better."

Wow, her friend knew her even better than she'd thought. "He seems like a really nice guy, and yeah…I'll admit he's cute. Not super-macho or anything, but still cute. And he was kind to offer his help." Okay, she'd better limit her talk about him, or Zoey would sense how appealing he really was to her.

"Hey, gotta go. Trevor's trying to call," Zoey said.

After Meg shut off her phone and cleaned her supper dishes, she shoved away thoughts of Helena's call. Instead, she allowed her mind to drift to a tall, lanky man with shaggy hair and a cute grin. Maybe when he helped her with the boxes, she'd get to know him better. Her stomach did flips at the possibility.

6

Todd stared at his recent bank statement. Would he ever be able to afford a house? He was so tired of living in the small apartment and was certain even Mozart would prefer more space. But that required a certain amount of money, and now that his substitute teaching job was almost finished, he would only have his piano tuning and his choir director pay, once that started.

Maybe he could do something else music-related, such as teach private music lessons. One thing was certain—he absolutely would not go to his aunt for financial help. Aunt Ellen would assist him in a heartbeat if she thought he needed it, but he refused to do that. After all, he was thirty-two years old and perfectly capable of providing for himself. And a cat.

But what about a wife? The silent reminder that he might be single forever resurfaced in his thoughts. After enduring the painful split with his ex-wife, he'd entertained the thought that someday he might remarry. But he wasn't going to rush into anything just for the sake of being married. No, this time he'd be certain his bride was the right woman for him, and that he was the right man, which apparently hadn't been the case for his ex-wife.

The image of Meg popped into his mind. Although she'd acted friendly toward him, would she ever date him? With her outgoing personality, she probably wasn't interested in an introvert. Other than a love of music, they had little in common. Well, except cats. When he'd tuned her piano, she'd mentioned her two cats. He could tell she adored them.

Okay—two things in common. Music and cats. But that wasn't enough to know if they'd be compatible—not by a long shot. In many ways they were polar opposites. Maybe when he helped her unpack books, he'd learn more about her. The ring of the phone jarred his musings.

"Todd? How are you, man?" The voice of his buddy in Birmingham was like an old, familiar song in his ears.

"Hey Chip. I'm good. I tried to phone you last week, but got your voice mail."

"Yeah, sorry about that. After we'd texted, I knew you were going to call, but we ended up visiting the in-laws and my phone was on silent. Then work got busy, so I'm finally returning your call." After asking about Todd's aunt and his work, Chip tossed out an unexpected question. "So how are things in the romance department, buddy? Are you seeing anyone special now? And just for the record, I think you're much better off without Tara."

Whoa. He'd not been prepared for their conversation to head in that direction so quickly. But Chip had good intentions, so Todd plunged forward and opened up to him.

"No, I'm not seeing anyone. But there's a nice lady named Meg who lives here in Coastal Breeze. I tuned her piano a while back, and since then have seen her at church. And also, when I took my aunt to the doctor, Meg happened to work in the office."

Chip laughed. "Well, that's convenient. Have you asked her out yet? If she's single and appeals to you, there's no need to waste time."

"Nah, I haven't asked her out. She's a widow—she told me that when I worked on her piano. But there's something about her…she's just really nice. And nice to look at, too."

"You didn't ask for my advice, but I'd suggest as soon as you have the chance, ask her out. If it turns out she's got a man in her life, she can tell you. But you'll never know unless you ask her."

"Yeah, you're right. I'm supposed to help her unpack books in the used bookstore she's opening, so hopefully then we'll talk more." Okay, time to get off the topic of Todd's love life, or lack thereof. "So, when are you coming to visit the Florida panhandle? It's beautiful here."

"That's the other reason I phoned you. Julie is planning a visit to see her old college roommate in Georgia, and she's taking Henry. You know, kind of a 'girls with kids' weekend. I thought if you're available that weekend, I'll head your way."

"Sounds great. Which weekend will it be?" Even though Todd knew he'd be available, he didn't want to sound totally pathetic.

Chip explained it would be in mid-May, and he'd drive down early Saturday and he'd return home to Birmingham on Sunday afternoon.

Todd assured him that was fine, and the friends talked a few more minutes before the call ended. After clicking off his phone, he realized how much he missed the times he and Chip used to hang out in Birmingham. Even after Chip had married, they'd kept in pretty close touch. Now that his friend had made the effort to rekindle their friendship, it was up to Todd to do his part.

As he fed Mozart and did a load of laundry, Todd realized he was genuinely looking forward to his friend's visit. At least hanging out with Chip for a weekend would be good for some laughs, and Todd hadn't done enough laughing in the past year.

~ ~ ~

After receiving the upsetting phone call from Helena, Meg hesitated before answering her phone when it rang the next day, but she ended up being glad she'd answered. The realtor phoned to say her bid had been accepted for the building space next door to Cindy Lou's Candy Shop, and Meg needed to meet with the owner on Saturday.

She could hardly believe it, and with trembling hands she phoned her parents to tell them. They were thrilled and offered encouragement to move ahead towards her goal. Then she phoned Zoey, who was ecstatic.

"I knew good things were headed your way,

girlfriend. You're due some really positive news after what you've been through, being widowed and then harassed by Cruella. And you know once your bookstore opens, I plan to be your first customer." She giggled and Meg's spirits soared. Yep, no doubt about it—Zoey had been the best friend she could've asked for.

"I'm so grateful for your support, Zoey, that I'll gladly give you some books for free." Was this all a dream and she'd awaken soon?

But this was real, and now she needed to get into high gear with her plans. For so long, the bookstore had been a long-distance dream, and she'd happily jotted notes on paper outlining how she'd run her business. Now it was becoming a reality, so no more daydreaming. Time to apply those plans and make her business a success once it was up and running.

Zoey chattered happily about taking Meg out to dinner to celebrate and offered to help any way that she could. Meg couldn't help thinking that a stranger listening to their conversation might think it was Zoey who was opening a business because of her unbridled excitement.

"You're so sweet, Zoey. I should be the one treating you to a dinner out, because you've been so encouraging. But I guess before we plan any kind of celebration, I'd better get things finalized."

"What about your job for Dr. Phipps? Will you be able to keep working there? I'll miss you like crazy if you're not there anymore."

"I've thought about that a lot, and I've already spoken to him about gradually cutting back on my hours while he searches for a new office manager. From my understanding, that's what he plans to do. My ultimate goal is to work in my bookstore full-time. I figure if I don't have it open very much, I'll never sell anything." She laughed, but knew her words held truth.

"Yeah, you're right. Well, even when you're not working for Dr. Phipps at all, we can still hang out and I'll visit your store." Zoey sounded a bit sentimental, so Meg wanted to lighten their talk.

"You'd better stay in touch with me. Besides, I'll still be in Coastal Breeze, so it's not like I'm opening a shop over in Tallahassee." Both women laughed.

After the call ended, Meg took out her planner and stared at the calendar page. At this point, she couldn't plan anything definite because she hadn't closed on the property yet. Nothing was actually finalized. *However, after this Saturday I'll be able to make definite plans. That is, if everything goes through. Of course it will,* she argued. *What could possibly put a wrench in her plans now that it was approved by the bank?*

With excitement running through her, she grabbed a pen and jotted more ideas for her used bookstore—her inventory, how she'd advertise, and special activities for her grand opening.

But amid her excitement, a subtle fear threatened to overshadow her good feelings. What if her store wasn't successful and she didn't sell many books? What if running her own business was much harder than she'd anticipated? This venture would be a tremendous responsibility, and she'd be in charge. What did she know about running a business anyway?

Besides fear, she had guilt poking at her, which didn't help. Was she making a mistake by leaving her position as office manager for Dr. Phipps? Would she regret giving up the security of a steady paycheck and insurance? Gradually the exhilaration from minutes earlier gave way to a feeling akin to despair.

Meg rose to her feet and drew in a deep breath. If it wasn't close to her bedtime, she'd be tempted to brew a small pot of coffee, but instead she stepped to her refrigerator for a glass of ice water. Maybe that would clear her mind and shove away the ridiculous fear taking over.

As she sipped the cold liquid, her eyes lit on a small plaque in her kitchen. Her mother had given it to Meg when she was in college. The Scripture was a reminder that she needed at that moment, so she read the words several times.

For God hath not given us the spirit of fear; but of power, and of love, and of a sound mind. Meg read the words again, letting them sink in and calm her spirit.

The Lord had allowed her dream to become a reality, so rather than be fearful and worry about what might go wrong, she needed to do her best and trust. Easier said than done, but she'd have to keep working at it. If she was ever going to move forward, she had to take those first steps. And trust.

~ ~ ~

Ellen's chipper voice came through the phone, and Todd couldn't suppress a smile at her enthusiasm. "I knew that when folks learned about a good piano tuner in the area, you'd have more jobs lined up, Toddles."

"Thanks to you helping to spread the word. I really appreciate your help." Todd was definitely not a salesman or good at advertising his own services. His aunt, on the other hand, was a born promoter—a natural social butterfly who knew lots of people in their community. Apparently, she wasn't timid about letting them know her nephew tuned pianos either.

"You know I'm happy to help my favorite nephew. Especially after what you've been through. I'm still tickled you made the move here from Birmingham."

"Yes, I am too, thanks to your encouragement." His gratitude was genuine. Aunt Ellen had helped him so much, especially after his parents passed away.

"Now catch me up on your job situation, dear. When do you begin as our church choir director? I've not been a part of the choir, but from what I've heard it's a very jovial group. They have holiday gatherings and enjoy fellowship from time to time."

Todd wasn't so sure how he felt about that, but didn't want to put a damper on his aunt's exuberance. After all, it wasn't her fault that he was an introvert.

"I begin in June. I'm a little nervous about taking over as the director. I'm still new in the church and don't know many people yet, and as you know, I'm not very assertive." He forced out a chuckle, relieved when his aunt laughed good-naturedly.

"You'll do just fine, Toddles. I have faith in you. Obviously, the pastor also has faith in you or he wouldn't have hired you."

Todd hadn't thought about it in that way, and he had to admit his aunt's perspective made him feel a bit better. Still, he hoped he wouldn't regret taking on this job.

"You're very kind. I'll do my best, and then if the church isn't pleased, they can hire someone else." He hated to sound so cut-and-dried about the matter, but that's all he could do.

Once again Ellen assured him that he'd be fine. But her next comment sent his pulse racing.

"Earl phoned me again, and he wants to see us before he heads back to Kentucky." Her words came to a halt—as though not wanting to upset Todd.

He felt a sickening in his gut. It wasn't from the pizza he'd eaten for supper, but more from being around his cousin again. Unsure what to say, he simply replied with, "Oh." He wasn't going to lie and say that was fine, because it wasn't. He had no desire to be around the relative who'd caused so much strife and pain in his life in the past.

"I thought I'd check with you first and see when you could meet for dinner. I'd prefer to meet at a restaurant as we did before. I just don't feel comfortable having Earl in my home."

Todd's previous suspicions had turned out to be valid. Although his aunt had given the excuse of redoing her living room, he'd known she didn't want to have the unstable relative in her house, and he didn't blame her.

"That's fine, Aunt Ellen. You just tell me when, and I'll pick you up and drive to the restaurant. We could eat at The Happy Fisherman again."

With obvious relief in her tone, she suggested the date and time. "I'll give Earl a quick call and let him know." She paused before continuing. "And Toddles, I know it's not easy for you being around him, but you're a good man. Hopefully, Earl will return to Kentucky soon, and we'll pray that he truly does have his life straightened out now."

After their call ended, Todd tried not to think about the upcoming meal with Earl, but instead focused on his duties as the choir director. And the more he thought about it, the more he realized he just might enjoy this position. At least his love of music would be put to use, and although the pay wasn't much, it would help.

His thoughts drifted from the church choir to a particular choir member. Would Meg continue being part of the choir when he took over? At least that would be an opportunity to see Meg on a regular basis, and get to know her better. He also wondered when she might need him to help unpack books in her shop.

Now if he could just get through another dinner with his cousin, he could focus on more positive thoughts. Thoughts regarding his new position as the choir director, and a certain choir member he hoped to see more often.

~ ~ ~

Dr. Phipps smiled at Meg, as if sensing she was nervous about their conversation. In a gentle tone, the middle-aged physician spoke words that endeared him to her. "Meg, remember you've got to do what's best for you. It sounds as though you've had a goal to have your own bookstore for quite a while, and now it's coming to fruition." He adjusted the glasses on his nose.

She offered a weak smile. "Yes, it's something I've dreamed about and worked toward for quite some time, Dr. Phipps. I'm just so torn, though, because I don't want to leave this job." Meg hoped he realized she was sincere.

"I'll find another office manager, although your replacement won't be nearly as competent as you, I'm sure. But please don't feel badly about leaving to work in your shop. I'm happy for you and wish you the best. Besides, it's not as though you abruptly quit and left me in a bind. You've given me plenty of notice so I could begin searching for another office manager." He reached out and gave her shoulder a fatherly pat.

For some strange reason, Meg felt she was about to cry. How embarrassing. She had to get in control of her emotions, so she forced a smile and nodded. "Thank you, Dr. Phipps. You're the best doctor and the best boss."

Their talk was brought to a close as Olga called to the doctor that his wife was on the line. "It's not an emergency, but she really needs to speak with you, if possible."

Dr. Phipps grinned and shook his head, then headed toward his private office. Meg took a deep breath, feeling relief and also something else—a tinge of sadness. She would miss this job, in addition to missing her co-workers. They had been wonderfully supportive when they'd learned she was a widow, and a bond had developed among the small staff.

As she organized some medical supplies in one of the examination rooms, Meg gave herself a silent pep talk. She'd still be in Coastal Breeze and could keep in touch with Dr. Phipps and his employees. Not to mention she and Zoey would still see each other, since they were best friends. It wasn't as if she was leaving the area to move far away.

Still, there was a certain amount of emotion involved in this major decision. But while she was still employed for Dr. Phipps, she needed to do the very best she could, even as she planned ahead for her business.

As Meg grabbed a quick cup of coffee that afternoon, the receptionist joined her in the breakroom. "Whew. I am so glad it's Friday, because I am beat." The heavy-set woman opened the employee refrigerator and grabbed a canned cola, then headed to the small table on one side of the room.

"Do you have special plans for the weekend?" Meg sipped her coffee and eyed the woman. Although she could be a bit dramatic at times, Olga was a good person, and Meg would miss her.

Olga cackled. "Special plans? Not unless you

call errands and cleaning house special plans." She grinned and winked at Meg. "But thank you for asking. What about you? Any big dates this weekend?"

To her surprise, Meg's mind immediately conjured an image of Todd. Which was ridiculous, since they weren't dating. Her face warming to a conspicuous pink, she shook her head and took another sip of coffee.

Instead of changing the subject, the receptionist stared at her with wide eyes. "You don't? I really figured you'd be dating someone—you're such an attractive young lady, and you've been widowed more than a respectable amount of time."

Meg almost choked on her coffee. Olga meant well. "Maybe one day, but so far I've been fine as a single woman again." She rinsed her coffee cup, eager to exit the breakroom and get back to work. Meg didn't care to discuss her single status with the woman, no matter how good her intentions were.

The receptionist smiled and spoke in a gentler tone. "Well, when the time is right, you'll know. And I feel certain there's a special man out there for you."

Unsure how to respond, Meg simply nodded and headed to the main office area. The ringing phone ensured that she wouldn't be questioned anymore by Olga—at least not that afternoon.

After the medical office closed, Meg and Zoey headed to their cars together. "Did I tell you I've rounded up more books for your store?" Zoey clicked her keypad to unlock her car.

"More books? Thanks, girlfriend. I really

appreciate that. You mentioned earlier in the week you'd been able to gather a box full, which is great."

"Yep. I got some from my aunt who's downsizing. She planned to give them away anyhow, so she was glad for me to take them."

"Please tell her I said thank you." Meg drew in a deep breath. She was again reminded that her bookstore was no longer a distant dream. It was becoming a reality, and she had much work ahead of her.

"I'm supposed to have a date with Trevor tomorrow night, but would you like to have lunch on Sunday after church? Or are you going to see your parents?"

Meg opened her car door but didn't climb inside yet. "No, Sunday lunch sounds good. Enjoy your date with Trevor." She didn't add what she was thinking. Hopefully Trevor wouldn't cancel, as he'd done more than a few times.

Driving to her cottage, Meg decided on a whim to stop by the local gift shop for a few minutes. She always enjoyed browsing Ginny's Treasures by the Sea and seeing what new products were displayed. Maybe she'd even find something else for her sister-in-law's expected baby, although she still wasn't sure if the baby was a girl or boy.

Entering the store minutes later, Meg was greeted by Ginny's southern drawl along with a delightful, citrusy scent. After returning a greeting to the older woman, Meg headed for the center of the shop, where shelves held eye-pleasing displays of figurines, candles, small framed prints, and much more.

As Meg was eyeing a small painting of a lighthouse, Ginny came toward her. "Sugar, did you need any help, or do you just want to browse?" The store owner wore a skirt and top that were a lovely shade of green, and her matching earrings and necklace made Meg think of an older model in a catalog.

"I'm just browsing, but thank you. By the way, what is that scent I smelled as I entered the store?" It had been pleasing without being too strong.

Ginny beamed and gestured toward a nearby shelf. "It's one of the new candles that arrived yesterday. I'm so excited about them, because they're already a favorite with customers. I've even purchased a few myself." She put a well-manicured hand to her mouth and giggled.

Meg smiled and nodded. "I can see how they're a favorite, because that scent is very pleasant." Meg reached for one, already deciding she'd purchase it to put with her mom's gifts for the upcoming Mother's Day holiday.

Then she reached for one of the small, lighthouse paintings. She smiled as she noticed the artist's name in the corner. Taking her items to the counter, she commented to Ginny. "I'm glad you're still selling Avril's paintings. How is she doing?" Meg had only met the young woman once, when she was visiting her brother Thomas and his wife, Emma.

Ginny beamed at the mention of Avril's name. "Oh, she is doing great. She's married now, and still amazes everyone at how well she gets around after being in a wheelchair for so long."

Meg smiled, glad to hear the update on the young woman, who'd been seriously injured in an automobile accident, but had made a miraculous recovery over time. "I hope Avril will continue painting, because her talent is amazing."

Ginny nodded in agreement, then surprised Meg with a question. "Are you excited about opening your bookstore, honey?" She handed Meg the wrapped items in a gift bag.

"Yes, ma'am. But I still have much work to do in preparation." Then a groove formed between her eyes. "Do you think many people have heard about it already? I haven't put any advertisements out yet. I'm still in the early stages of preparing."

Ginny patted her hand and offered a warm smile. "Since this is a small, close-knit community, nothing stays secret for long. I think it's wonderful, and I'm excited to have a used bookstore in our area."

Her comments reassured Meg and offered hope that her little business would be well-received. Because when she allowed her mind to think of all she still needed to do, it was overwhelming.

~ ~ ~

The Happy Fisherman restaurant wasn't terribly crowded, to Todd's relief. He hoped that meant they'd be served in a timely manner and wouldn't need to stay too long. He still didn't trust Earl. What were his real motives for coming to Coastal Breeze?

"Maybe we should go ahead and be seated, and we can watch for Earl from our table." Ellen suggested as they stood inside the doorway of the restaurant.

The hostess led them to a table where they had a clear view of the door.

Todd hated the way his pulse raced, and he rubbed sweaty palms against his pantlegs. He tried to tell himself that the previous meal with Earl had gone well, with no incidents. So why shouldn't this time go as smoothly? Still, his gut was never wrong, and it was clearly warning him to be on guard around his cousin.

After five minutes, Ellen waved toward Earl when he entered the restaurant. He made his way toward them, looking more unkempt than he had before. When he joined them, he smiled. "Hello, good to see you both again."

The moment his cousin spoke, Todd caught the distinct stench of alcohol, and noticed Earl's eyes were glassy and red. *Not a good sign.* Todd hoped his cousin wouldn't cause a scene. His aunt certainly didn't need that.

"Are you still heading back to Kentucky tomorrow, Earl?" Ellen asked as she opened her menu.

Earl hesitated. After a few seconds of silence, he shrugged. "Yeah, I guess I'll drive back tomorrow. That is, if my old car makes it. My buddy from the motel gave me a ride here today." He released a cackle that turned a few heads in the restaurant, and Todd inwardly cringed.

Ellen must've picked up on Earl's current state

too because she tapped his menu and encouraged him to decide what he wanted to eat. "This is my treat." She shot a look at Todd, her narrowed eyes telling him not to argue.

Given the circumstances, it would be best to keep things as low-key as possible, so he simply nodded. He would repay her later because he certainly didn't expect a retiree to buy his meals.

After they'd placed their orders with the server, Ellen continued the conversation. "Do you have a job lined up in Kentucky, or will you need to job-hunt when you return?" She took a sip of her tea, her eyes holding a hint of worry that Todd didn't miss.

Earl ran a hand over his unshaven face. "I don't know what I'll do yet. But nope, don't have no job waitin' for me." Before anyone else could comment, Earl turned his gaze on Todd. "I'm surprised you live by the ocean, cousin. I didn't think you liked water." A gleam in his eyes sent Todd's defenses into overdrive. He remembered that same taunting look from years ago.

Doing his best to appear calm, Todd replied matter-of-factly. "I love living here, and the ocean is beautiful." He wished their food would arrive. At least when Earl was eating he wouldn't pepper him with unwanted questions or comments.

Earl shrugged as his eyes darted between Todd and Ellen. "I just remembered you didn't like that lake when we were teens, so I figured you wouldn't want to live near any water."

Before Todd could reply, Ellen spoke in a forceful tone. "As Todd said, the ocean here is beautiful. If you haven't had a good look at our beach yet, you really should before you return to Kentucky. Ah, here comes our food." She sent a knowing smile to Todd.

"Smells delicious." Todd eyed the seafood platters, determined to enjoy his food the best he could under the circumstances. He should've known his cousin would eventually bring up the past. Apparently, young bullies grew into old bullies.

The remainder of their time at the restaurant passed uneventfully, with light conversation about the weather and the upcoming summer season bringing more traffic to the area. Todd was grateful to his aunt for making sure Earl didn't have opportunities to bring up the past again.

"Are you men ready to leave?" Ellen smiled as she began to rise from her chair.

"Yes, and thank you again for the wonderful meal, Aunt Ellen." Todd smiled as he assisted with her chair.

Earl simply nodded and grunted out a subdued "thanks" as he stood. His eyes darted around the restaurant. Did he realize how unkempt he looked?

"Is your friend coming to pick you up?" Ellen asked. Todd hoped his cousin wouldn't need a ride in his car.

Earl waved his cell phone and nodded. "Yeah, I just gotta phone him. He'll be here soon."

"Okay, good. Have a safe drive back to Kentucky, Earl." Ellen gave him a quick hug, and Todd shook his cousin's hand. Earl barely made eye contact with him.

Todd and his aunt got into his car to leave. He

couldn't help releasing a long sigh of relief that the meal was over. He only hoped he wouldn't have more encounters with Earl, although he still wasn't convinced that his cousin was, in fact, returning to Kentucky the next day. Time would tell.

Ellen reached over and patted his arm as he started the car. "I know this wasn't easy for you, Todd, and I'm sorry Earl brought up the past. He'd obviously had alcohol before joining us today, don't you think?" Her lips pursed.

"I'm afraid he had. I could smell it on him, plus his eyes were bloodshot. He should have more respect for you." Todd shook his head, tamping down feelings of angry frustration.

"Yes, I noticed too. I'm glad he's not driving today. And I really don't think he would've brought up the past if he hadn't been drinking before he arrived. Alcohol gives some people a false sense of courage, I've heard." She shook her head. "Such a shame. Earl has loving parents who have always given him all the opportunities he could've wanted, but he squandered everything and made a mess of his life."

Echoing the mood of their conversation, the sun went behind some clouds, causing the previously bright day to become darkened. Was a storm approaching?

After Todd escorted his aunt into her home, he heard a rumble of thunder. "No wonder the sun disappeared. It sounds as though we're in for a storm. You weren't planning on going out again today, were you?" He glanced around his aunt's cozy cottage, silently wishing his own residence was as inviting. One day he'd be in a house—before too long.

Ellen grinned as she put on water for tea. "No, dear. I'm home and have plenty to keep me busy. Do you want to stay for a cup of tea or coffee?"

Todd thanked her but declined. "Mozart has never liked thunder, so I'd better return to my apartment and check on him. I'm going to go over some music I hope to use with the choir after I become the director."

His aunt beamed at him and Todd saw the pride in her eyes. She was tickled that her nephew would soon be leading the music in the church she loved. They hugged, and then Todd drove to his apartment, but his thoughts kept returning to the uncomfortable meal with Earl. Instead of his cousin, he needed to focus on his jobs and getting his finances in order so he could purchase a house.

With a stab of guilt poking at him, he realized he also needed to pray. Pray about his work situations, his finances, and Earl. Regardless of Todd's feelings about his wayward cousin, the man had serious issues, and could use prayers.

~ ~ ~

The following Monday morning, Dr. Phipps's office was unusually busy. It seemed that quite a few local folks were battling allergy problems and other medical issues. Meg knew she mustn't allow her mind to daydream about her bookstore, because she needed to focus on the patients and keep things running smoothly. She also didn't need to think about seeing Todd in church the previous day. To her disappointment, she couldn't chat with him because several choir members continued talking to her after they left the loft. By the time she headed outside, most of the congregation had dispersed—including the handsome piano tuner.

"Whew. I hope things will slow down this afternoon." Olga shook her head as she reached for the ringing phone—yet again. The phone had rung constantly that morning, and Meg had taken calls on the secondary line while Olga handled calls on the main line.

Meg nodded at the receptionist's complaint, yet couldn't help but think that staying busy had its perks. She couldn't imagine having a job so slow that she watched the clock at every opportunity. Her mind switched gears to her planned bookstore. Fear weaseled into her thoughts. Would it be slow at her store? Would she even have enough customers to make a go of it?

"Meg, would you please assist me in room three?" Dr. Phipps's voice cut into her thoughts and she silently chided herself. She could think about her business later because her job was here, and it didn't allow for mistakes—not where human health was concerned.

"Yes, sir." She hurried to the examination room at the end of the short hallway and stepped inside to see a little girl and a woman who appeared to be her mother. The child appeared terrified as she sat on the exam table, her mother hovering next to her.

"Hello there. My name is Meg and I'm going

to help Dr. Phipps. What's your name?" Meg offered a cheerful smile—first to the child and then the adult.

The little girl nibbled her bottom lip, her eyes welling with tears. The woman introduced herself as Shelly Iverson, and her child's name was Nicole. Then she leaned closer to whisper. "She's usually not this shy, but she's very nervous right now. I think she has an ear infection."

"It's nice to meet you both, and I'm sorry you're not feeling well today, Nicole. But Dr. Phipps is a very good doctor, so I'm sure you'll be feeling better soon." Meg noticed the child clasped a book tightly to her chest, as though squeezing it gave her comfort.

"Did you bring a book with you?" Meg didn't recognize it as one they kept in the waiting area.

Nicole barely nodded, so her mother answered for the child. "Yes, that's Nicole's favorite book—or at least one of them. She loves books."

Meg brightened and exclaimed. "Oh, I love books too, Nicole. In fact…" She lowered her voice as if telling a secret. "I'm going to open a used bookstore soon. And I'll have lots of books for children, so maybe sometime you and your mom can stop by." Meg resisted the urge to giggle when the child raised her head and a tiny smile crept onto her face.

"How special. Your very own bookstore?" Shelly looked surprised.

"Yes, ma'am. The books for sale will be used books, rather than brand-new. But they'll be in good condition and less expensive than new books. I'm excited about doing this, because it's been my dream for a while." Dr. Phipps's footsteps approached, so she stopped talking about her store.

"Here's Dr. Phipps now." Meg grinned at Nicole and her mother, then assisted the physician as he checked the child's ears and vital signs. But during her examination, the little girl kept directing her gaze to Meg, and the hint of a smile played on her mouth.

Once the doctor diagnosed an ear infection and wrote a prescription, he exited the small room to check on the next patient. Meg stayed behind to visit with Nicole and her mother a few more minutes.

"I hope you'll feel better soon, Nicole. The medicine Dr. Phipps gave you should help." She didn't miss the appreciative look from the child's mother.

"Thank you." Nicole timidly squeaked out a reply, still clasping her book.

"We'll plan to visit your bookstore when it opens. Where will it be located?" Shelly helped her daughter off the exam table and then smiled at Meg.

"On Palm Street, next to Cindy Lou's Candy store." She suppressed a laugh when Nicole's head jerked up at the mention of candy.

"I know exactly where that is, so we'll be certain to stop in after you've opened. And I hope your store does very well." As the trio headed out of the exam room, Shelly leaned over to Meg and whispered. "Thanks for being so sweet to my daughter."

Meg grinned. "I'm sorry she's sick, but it was

nice meeting you both."

As she tidied the exam room for the next patient, Meg thought about the sweet child she'd just met. Would she ever have a daughter of her own, or maybe a son? The thought sent her heart leaping, although nothing in her life indicated that was close to happening.

Zoey stepped up to her as she left the exam room. "Did you already know the lady and little girl who just left? They seemed to like you."

Meg shook her head. "No, I'd never met them before today, but the child and mom were both super nice. And the daughter loves books, so I told them about my bookstore."

With a gentle, playful punch to Meg's arm, Zoey shook her head and laughed. "With your friendly personality, I have no doubt you'll have plenty of customers in your shop." Before Zoey could say more, the receptionist called to her with a question about a patient.

Meg went on with her routine duties, keeping an ear tuned for Dr. Phipps's voice in case he needed her assistance again. Yet Zoey's words hovered in her thoughts. Would Meg actually have plenty of customers in her bookstore, or would it be a struggle getting folks to visit her small business?

Olga's voice speaking with Dr. Phipps snapped her back to the present. The name of Ellen Davis was mentioned, and Meg went on high alert, hoping Todd's aunt wasn't sick again.

~ ~ ~

"No worries, Aunt Ellen. I'll swing by Dr. Phipps's office and pick up your prescription on my way home. I should be able to leave the school at three o'clock. Are you sure you don't need it sooner?"

"That will be fine, Toddles. You're such a dear helping me out. Since my pesky cough has returned, I'm hesitant to get out and have a coughing fit, otherwise I'd drive and pick it up myself." As if emphasizing her comment, her cough rattled through the phone.

Promptly at three o'clock, Todd headed out. Would he see Meg when he stopped at the doctor's office? He was certain as the office manager she always had plenty to do, so she'd likely be tied up when he arrived.

Entering the waiting room, he noticed most of the seats were taken by people waiting to be seen. He headed to the window to check in. Employees were scurrying around in the back. Must be a busy afternoon. He hated to interrupt anyone, yet wanted to get his aunt's prescription so he could have it filled at the pharmacy. He cleared his throat.

A plump woman with a pleasant smile approached the window. "Yes, may I help you?"

Before Todd could state what he needed, Meg rushed toward the woman. "Thanks, Olga. I've got this." She grinned at the woman.

Meg didn't step to the window, but instead came from the office area out into the waiting room, standing mere inches from Todd. The fresh, floral scent he'd noticed the day they talked in the grocery store wafted toward him. He breathed in, then roused himself. He needed to focus on his reason for being there.

"You're here for Miss Ellen's prescription, right?" Meg peered up at him, her blue eyes gazing directly into his, almost taking his breath away. What was wrong with him?

"Um, yes. She asked me to pick up her prescription."

Meg handed it to him, and their hands touched briefly, just as they'd done that day in the grocery store.

"Thanks. Is there anything I need to tell my aunt?"

Meg shook her head. "No, the instructions will be on the bottle, but please remind her that this cough medicine is likely to cause drowsiness, so I'd advise not driving after taking a dose."

"Got it. I'll tell her. Thanks so much." The office was busy so he needed to leave. Yet his feet remained rooted to the spot.

Meg didn't appear to be in a hurry to leave either, because she stood looking up at him, smiling. "It's good to see you again. I heard you're going to be our new choir director beginning in June. That's great." Then she lowered her voice and leaned a tiny bit closer. "Will you still be able to help me unpack books when I'm setting up my bookstore?" Her eyes widened as she awaited his reply.

Todd nodded and grinned. "Absolutely. Just let me know when you need help." Before he could say more, a nurse called to Meg to assist with a patient. Just as well. His aunt was waiting for her medicine.

He had no business standing here visiting with the pretty office manager.

"Sorry, gotta go. See you later, Todd." Meg flashed a sweet smile, lifted a hand, and turned to head back to the office area. But she stopped, whirled around, and said, "Please tell Miss Ellen I hope she's better soon." She locked eyes with his for a few seconds, then Todd nodded and thanked her.

He drove to his aunt's pharmacy, then delivered the cough medicine to her home, yet all the while his thoughts remained on Meg. Had he imagined it, or did she feel an attraction to him too? There was no doubt he was flattered that she'd requested his help with unpacking books. During that time together he'd learn more about her. But would she enjoy his company? It was obvious they were on opposite ends of the personality scale.

Okay, so maybe the more he was around her, the less awkward he'd feel. After all, when he'd first begun dating Tara, he had been quite shy and withdrawn.

Ugh. He shoved away thoughts of his ex-wife. Not only did he not want to think about her and his failed marriage, but Meg Mills was in a totally different class from Tara. No comparison at all.

~ ~ ~

Meg went about the next few days wondering if she was dreaming at times. Knowing her bookstore would soon be a reality continued to bring both excitement and fear in her emotions—a constant battle inside that left her shell-shocked.

"Girlfriend, are you okay? You seem a little distracted today." Zoey eyed her closely as they ate lunch in the breakroom.

Meg nodded. "Yeah, I'm fine, but thanks for asking. Just have my mind on preparations for the bookstore, but while I'm still employed here, I want to do everything I need to do." She grabbed her bottled water and took a slow sip.

"Well, remember I'm available to help you. It's not as though I have a husband and children to hurry home to." Zoey blew out a sigh and rolled her eyes.

Had something happened? Meg questioned her friend, concerned that her relationship with Trevor had worsened. "Are you okay? Any updates on your relationship with Trevor?"

"I'm good, and there are no updates with Trevor—which is frustrating. I'm giving our relationship until Mother's Day weekend, and then I'm telling him we need to talk. If he has no interest in settling down in the next year, then we'll go our separate ways."

"That sounds like a good idea. You've been more than patient with him, and it's not like you're teens." Meg patted her friend's arm. "Keep me updated, okay?" She offered a smile, hoping that Trevor would get his act together and mature. Zoey didn't deserve to be strung along.

Later that afternoon, Meg arrived home from work and on a whim decided to walk on the beach. The springtime sunshine was warm, yet there was a breeze stirring, thanks to the gulf. She knew with the approaching summer season, there would be more tourists with each coming week. Although she was an extrovert, Meg preferred her beach walks to be calm and relaxing, without throngs of beachgoers around her.

When she parked her car and headed toward the beach minutes later, she breathed in the salty air, the misty breeze instantly refreshing her face. To her relief, there were only a few other people walking, scattered here and there along the water's edge. For a few minutes, Meg allowed her mind to block out thoughts of all she needed to accomplish. She watched the seagulls perform their smooth glides and touch on the water's surface to grab a fish. Today the water appeared a shade of teal—one of Meg's favorite colors. She continued her walk a little further, and was about to turn around and retrace her steps when she noticed a tall man walking alone.

He wasn't at the water's edge, but rather further inland strolling in the sand. She squinted in the late day sunshine, and then realized his identity. Todd. Had he noticed her?

Meg headed toward him, veering away from the water. A small smile played against his lips, and he lifted his hand in a slight wave. "Hi, Meg."

Approaching within two feet of him, Meg gazed up into his gray eyes and grinned. "Hi, Todd. How's Miss Ellen feeling? Is her cough getting better?"

He nodded his head. "She's a little better, thanks for asking. I think that cough syrup is helping."

"I'm glad. Please tell her to rest and if she needs Dr. Phipps, don't hesitate to phone."

"Okay, I'll tell her." He glanced toward the parking lot.

"I guess you're heading home, so I won't keep you. I need to get some more walking in before the sun sets. This beach is beautiful, isn't it? I can see why this area is called the Emerald Coast." She laughed lightly, but noticed the subtle shadow that covered his eyes when she glanced toward the ocean.

"Yeah, it's a...pretty area." After a few beats of silence, he looked again toward the parking lot. "Just let me know when you need my help in your bookstore. See you later." He lifted a hand in a wave, then turned and walked toward his car.

Meg resisted the urge to turn around and watch him walk away. She'd been tempted to ask him if he ever walked at the water's edge, but had decided not to. Yet it was obvious that he kept as far away as possible from the lapping water. Oh well, maybe he just preferred to keep his feet dry.

Ten more minutes of walking at the water's edge and Meg returned to her car and headed home. The walk had refreshed her—helped to clear the jumbled thoughts about her bookstore and what she needed to accomplish.

Not to mention, she was glad to see Todd again, and he'd mentioned helping in her bookstore. Such a kind man—caring and attentive to his elderly aunt, and offering to help Meg although they didn't know each other well.

Yet Meg couldn't deny hoping that would

change. She'd like very much to know the shaggy-haired piano tuner better. Then maybe she could discover the reason for the shadow in his gray eyes.

7

When Todd returned to his apartment after his walk on the beach, all he could think about was seeing Meg. In retrospect, maybe he should've turned around and continued walking—with her. After all, there was no rush for him to get back to his apartment. Mozart was fine, and that would've been a good opportunity to spend a little time with Meg.

His phone rang as he finished a sandwich. Aunt Ellen's number was displayed on the caller ID. He hoped the medicine he'd picked up earlier in the week was still helping her.

"Hello, Toddles. Are you busy?" Ellen's voice held a hint of hoarseness.

"No, Aunt Ellen. I just finished supper. How are you feeling?" Although he needed to shower since his skin felt sticky from the mist and sand at the beach, he'd hop in his car right away if she needed anything.

"I'm fine, and I wanted to thank you again for picking up my prescription the other day. You're the best nephew." She hesitated and cleared her throat. "There's another reason I'm calling you, dear."

Oh no. Todd didn't like the sound of this, and his grip tightened on the phone. He waited for her to explain.

"It's about Earl. As it turns out, he hasn't left for Kentucky yet, so he's still in the area."

Todd's gut reacted immediately. Good thing he'd only eaten a sandwich rather than a large meal. He'd assumed his cousin had returned to Kentucky days earlier. Wishful thinking. Resisting the urge to groan, Todd replied. "I didn't realize that. Has he been calling you again?" He still didn't trust Earl.

"Yes, he phoned yesterday to say he'd had car trouble and was still at the motel. Then he phoned again today, wanting to know if he could visit me." A coughing spell followed her words.

Todd waited until her coughing had subsided, then he spoke firmly. "Aunt Ellen, I hope you didn't let him visit your house."

"No, dear. Part of me feels a bit guilty at not inviting him here, but as I've said before, given his past I just don't feel comfortable. Since I've had this bad cough, I told Earl that I've been sick and wouldn't want him to get my germs. He seemed to accept my excuse for not inviting him."

Todd was relieved, yet knew there was more. He held his breath waiting for her to continue.

After another lighter coughing spell, Ellen spoke again. "Anyway, he told me he was sorry I've been sick. Then he started talking about needing money and how he's trying to do better. He even said he regrets some bad choices he's made and knows he can do better but he needs money to start over."

Todd's heart raced as anger mounted. "I hope you didn't tell him you'd give him money, Aunt Ellen. I know that's your decision, but I don't want Earl taking advantage of your kindness."

"No, I didn't tell him I'd give him money. If I knew he was truly headed in the right direction, I'd help him. But my gut feeling is that he'd use the money for alcohol or something else he clearly doesn't need." Ellen's cough worsened and she sounded tired. "I told him to have a safe drive back to Kentucky, and that I'm praying for him. That was it. Hopefully he will return there soon."

"I think you did the right thing, so maybe he will leave the area. Are you certain he doesn't know where you live? I don't want him to show up at your door." Todd almost shuddered at the thought of a drunken Earl standing at his aunt's door, playing on her sympathy.

She assured him that Earl didn't know her address. "I just wanted to update you. I'd better stop talking now and take another dose of medicine."

"Okay. But promise me you'll phone me right away if you need anything."

With her promise, their call ended. Todd prayed that his aunt wouldn't be bothered by the wayward relative again. He also said a prayer for his cousin, because although Earl had caused pain and strife in Todd's past, he was obviously a troubled man. Todd prayed he wouldn't bring trouble to his aunt's life by remaining in the area.

~ ~ ~

Meg was eager to set an opening date for her bookstore, yet she still had much to do. When her father accompanied her to the building where her store would be located, she could hardly believe it was happening. They stepped inside and Meg gazed around at the empty space, visualizing where she'd place her shelves.

"Are you pleased with this space, Meggy?" Her father squeezed her arm.

She reached up and hugged him. "Yes, Dad, this should be perfect. And I appreciate your support so much. Being with me at the bank, and now coming here today means a lot. I know Mom is supportive too." Meg was reminded again of how blessed she was to have loving parents.

Her father nodded. "Yes, and you can be sure your mother would've come along with me today if she wasn't fighting a virus. But she'll be eager to see it when you have things set up."

After the papers were signed and details were discussed, the building's owner handed Meg the keys. "Congratulations, Meg. I hope you'll be very successful with your new business." The older man shook both their hands. Meg blushed as her father praised her to the landlord. She may not have given her parents a grandchild yet, but she would be the owner of a business. A burst of satisfaction traveled through her.

After the landlord left, Meg and her father stayed a bit longer so she could point out how she planned to have the store arranged. Before they left, a woman knocked at the door and peered through the glass. She looked familiar.

When Meg opened the door, the dark-haired woman beamed and thrust a package toward her. "You must be Meg. I'm Cindy Lou, the owner of the candy shop next door. Since we'll be neighbors, I wanted to welcome you with some fudge. I hope you'll enjoy it."

A warmth flooded Meg as she humbly took the box of fudge. The rich aroma drifted to her nose, and she could hardly wait to bite into the delicious treat. Cindy Lou's candy had always been her favorite.

Unexpected tears formed behind her eyelids. She was genuinely touched by this act of kindness. "Thank you so much, Cindy Lou. I'm Meg Mills, by the way, and this is my dad. I've been in your candy store several times, but one of your workers has assisted me, so you and I haven't actually met."

Cindy Lou seemed pleased. "Well, I hope you'll do very well with your bookstore, and I look forward to getting to know you better. I'd better run on back since I'm the only one working in my shop right now." She nodded at Meg's father and scurried out the door.

For a few seconds, Meg and her dad looked at each other. "That was really nice of her, wasn't it, Meggy?" He eyed the box hungrily.

"It sure was, Dad. Here, let's sample a piece before we leave, but I want you to take some home with you. Maybe this treat will help Mom feel better." Since Cindy Lou had placed several napkins inside the fudge box, Meg wrapped her fudge in those, and told her father to take the remaining pieces home in the box.

After locking the vacant store, Meg hugged her dad and climbed into her car to head to her cottage. Everything that was happening dazed her. Since things were now official, it was a matter of setting up her bookstore and getting the word out that she was open for business. Advertising would be the easy part. What she needed to do beforehand was daunting.

She was not only tired from putting in almost a full day at Dr. Phipps's office, but then hurrying to meet her father and the building owner to finalize the rental agreement. Thankfully, she'd gotten her business license earlier in the week with her father's assistance. With each item checked off her list, Meg moved closer to opening her store.

After feeding her cats, she ate supper and then phoned Zoey. She knew her friend would be eager for an update. Sure enough, Zoey answered on the first ring.

"Tell me everything, girlfriend. I could hardly focus on the patients after you left the office this afternoon. Are you pleased with the building space? Do you know about when you'll be opening?"

With Zoey's rapid-fire questions, Meg wondered if her friend had been drinking coffee, but knew that wasn't likely. Meg giggled despite her tiredness as she heard the enthusiasm in Zoey's voice.

"No opening date set yet, but I'm very happy with the space. I cannot wait to get my shelves situated and start placing the books—that will be the fun part. And also setting up a small area for children. Oh Zoey, there's so much I want to do, but I know it'll take time." Meg blew out a breath as her mind whirled.

"You'll get it done, and remember I'm always ready to help you."

Meg's eyes watered with unshed tears at her friend's comments. Zoey truly was the best friend she could have. But why did Meg feel so emotional today? She figured it must be the fact that she was finally realizing her dream. A dream she'd had for years—even before she'd married Roy.

Not wanting her friend to know how emotional she was, Meg forced an upbeat tone. "You know that you and my parents have been my biggest supporters with this." She paused and dabbed at her eyes, trying not to sniffle into the phone. "Since we both have to work tomorrow, I guess we'd better get off the phone now. Just don't let me get preoccupied with my bookstore in Dr. Phipps's office, okay? I need to focus while I'm still there." Zoey assured her that she'd keep her focused.

After the call ended, Meg prepared her clothes and lunch for the following day, but her mind remained on her bookstore. Her thoughts drifted to how things would be when she opened for business, and she tried to imagine welcoming customers into her small store.

But first, there were many details to handle and work to be done—including unpacking countless books. That sent her thoughts scurrying to Todd, since he'd agreed to help her. A tingle rushed through Meg as she thought of working side-by-side, unpacking books with Todd.

No doubt she was highly attracted to him. But was the feeling mutual?

~ ~ ~

Todd knew that the only way he could possibly purchase a house—even a bungalow with minimum square footage—would be to use some of his inheritance money from his late parents. He'd tried to leave the money in the bank and get by on his earnings, no matter how small. But staring at the written facts on paper showed him clearly what he'd have to do.

His future earnings as the church choir director combined with tuning jobs were not even close to the amount he'd need to purchase a home. Besides, he had no way of predicting how many people would need their pianos tuned in the coming months—after all, not everyone in the Florida panhandle area owned a piano.

He released a sigh and ran his fingers through his hair, which only served to remind him that he needed a haircut. Another expense, albeit a very small one. He blew out another sigh of frustration and almost jumped when Mozart leaped into his lap. The cat's purrs offered a bit of soothing comfort, and Todd couldn't suppress a smile.

Stroking the feline's soft fur, he gently spoke to his four-pawed companion. "Don't worry, fella. I'll always have money to buy food for you." As if completely understanding Todd's words, Mozart gazed up with his yellow-green eyes and purred like a motor.

After sitting a few more minutes and analyzing his financial situation, Todd was certain that he'd need to contact the Birmingham bank about withdrawing some of his inheritance money. He felt the familiar pang of sadness that always accompanied memories of his parents. Although they'd been gone over five years, he still missed them and knew he always would. Yet he had no doubt they would want the best for him, and he was certain if they could advise him right now, they'd tell him to use the funds he needed for a house.

His ringing phone pulled him from his thoughts and also prompted Mozart to leap from his lap onto the floor. "Sorry, fella." Todd grabbed his phone with one hand and gave the cat another gentle pat with the other.

He was glad to hear his buddy's voice on the line, and was reminded he was coming for a visit soon. "Hey, is your visit still on?" Todd was genuinely looking forward to seeing his good friend again.

"Sure thing, if that date still works for you. I'm looking forward to it. Besides, I've got a hankering for some fresh seafood." A hearty laugh followed Chip's comment, and Todd couldn't resist grinning.

The two men chatted for a few more minutes, finalizing the weekend plans and getting caught up on each other's routine schedules. Todd couldn't deny a longing as he listened to his friend describe the latest antics of his toddler son. He also mentioned his wife and laughed as he relayed stories of her experiments with various recipes. Yes, Chip seemed content with his married life, no doubt about it. Would Todd ever have that?

After their call ended, Todd's mind replayed his friend's comments. Then his thoughts switched to his first marriage. At the time, he'd figured he would end up staying married and having a couple of children. Not even close. Tara had turned out to be a completely different person than the woman he'd thought he had married. He never wanted to go through that again.

So why did he keep thinking about Meg? Someone who was obviously his polar opposite in personality and had so much to offer. Her friendliness to him most likely was only that—she was simply being herself. Yet Todd had told himself that she might be attracted to him, and that's why she'd been so nice. Who was he fooling? Besides, how could he guard his heart if he entertained thoughts of Meg having an attraction to him?

Opening his piano, Todd began playing several of his favorite hymns. He needed to prepare to lead the church choir in a few weeks and also line up more tuning jobs. That's where his mind should be, rather than wondering about his chances at a relationship with Meg.

On Saturday, Todd was glad to have another piano tuning job on the outskirts of Coastal Breeze. To his relief, the older couple didn't try to visit while Todd worked, so he was able to complete the task, receive his payment, and leave. He phoned his aunt to see if she needed anything while he was out.

"You're so thoughtful, Toddles, but I'm fine. I bought groceries yesterday and don't need a thing. You just enjoy your free time this weekend, because when you take over as the new choir director, you'll be busier, I'm sure." Ellen laughed good-naturedly.

Driving home, Todd replayed his aunt's comment. Surely the choir wouldn't consume all his weekend time, would it? Not that he had much else to do on his weekends. Although his aunt hadn't needed anything from the store, Todd decided to pick up more cat food and a few other items while he was out.

The store was situated at one end of Coastal Breeze, and despite the fact it wasn't a large chain store, it did a surprising amount of business. Each time Todd stopped by, customers filled the store. He made a mental list of what he needed, hoping this errand wouldn't take long.

As he went down the aisle with cat food, he remembered encountering Meg in this section of the store. It was kind of funny how they kept seeing each other—on the beach, the grocery store, and at church. Yet Coastal Breeze was a small community, so Todd shouldn't be surprised at their frequent encounters.

After placing a dozen cans of cat food in his shopping cart, Todd headed up the aisle to finish his shopping, but realized he'd been so preoccupied with thoughts of Meg that he didn't even remember what else he needed in the store. Good grief. He needed to stop thinking of the attractive woman and focus on his errand.

But driving home with his groceries twenty

minutes later, Todd couldn't deny that he hoped to see Meg at church the next morning. And maybe this time he'd have something important to say, rather than grinning at her like a lovesick teen.

~ ~ ~

"It sounds like everyone is in agreement with your suggestion of a choir picnic, Meg. When you mentioned it to me, I loved the idea, so I figured the others would too. Since Trevor has actually been more attentive lately, I'm going to invite him. But I'm not holding my breath that he'll be able to attend." Zoey laughed, sounding more upbeat to Meg than she had in a while.

"I hope he can come with you. And besides, just think of all the yummy food we'll have. Church functions are the best for homemade food." Meg giggled, already thinking ahead to the dishes she planned on preparing.

The friends left the choir room and headed through the worship area to exit the building. As they approached the main door to leave, Zoey nudged Meg with her elbow.

"Look. There's Todd, so why don't we go ahead and tell him about the choir picnic? He needs to know ahead of time in case there's a conflict with the date." Zoey stepped up her pace.

Meg nodded, hating the fact that her pulse raced as they drew closer to him. Would he think her forward? She drew in a deep breath and smiled. "Hi, Todd."

He immediately turned around and grinned at

both women. "Hi." He fidgeted with his church bulletin. "The choir sounded good."

Never the shy one, Zoey said, "Thanks, but we'll sound better when you are our director. No offense to dear Mr. Randall." She glanced around the room.

Since Todd appeared embarrassed by Zoey's comment, Meg filled the awkward gap by telling him about the picnic. "If the weather doesn't cooperate that day, we'll re-schedule. But we decided we'd better go ahead and set a date or the weeks will fly by. Please say you'll come. It's our way of welcoming you." Meg hoped she hadn't overwhelmed him.

Todd cast a quick glance at the ground, then returned his gaze to Meg. "Thank you, but the choir doesn't need to do anything special for me."

"We really want to do this. Besides, this will be a good way for you to meet the choir members." Zoey spoke in her usual enthused tone.

"Okay. Let me know what I need to bring and where the picnic will be held." Todd appeared as though he was more than ready to leave.

Zoey gave the location of the picnic, then Meg chimed in. "You'll be the guest of honor, so you won't need to bring anything. Except yourself." Meg giggled, then felt silly at her added comment. But when Todd's eyes met hers again, Meg's stomach flipped.

They said good-bye, then Todd hurried toward the parking area. Meg and Zoey remained on the walkway near the church building for a few more minutes, chatting. Yet Meg had to force herself to stay attentive to what her friend was saying, because her mind was stuck on the tall, lanky man she'd spoken with a few minutes earlier.

Her main thought was a question, but she didn't want to mention it to Zoey. No, she wasn't ready for her friend to know how attracted she was to Todd. Yet it puzzled her. Why had he appeared less than pleased when the picnic's location was mentioned? A lake was a typical spot for a gathering, but he looked almost panic-stricken. Meg couldn't help wondering why.

~ ~ ~

Todd was not looking forward to the choir picnic—especially since *he* was to be the guest of honor. He was starting to wonder if maybe he'd made a mistake by accepting the position as choir director. Yet what better job for someone who loved music as he did? Besides, the Coastal Breeze church wasn't huge, so it wasn't as though he'd be overseeing a choir of sixty people. Most Sundays he'd counted right around twenty-four choir members, and sometimes less.

"Mr. Davis, are you gonna teach us that new song today?" An eager third-grader questioned when it was time for class to begin.

Todd knew he needed to push away thoughts of becoming a choir director and focus on completing the school year with his young charges. Several other teachers at the elementary school had warned him that the closer summer drew, the livelier the students' behavior. He was already finding this to be true, and they still had two weeks to go.

He immersed himself in teaching a song to the youngsters, pleased when they caught on quicker than he'd expected. Todd was amazed at how time sped past. Thankfully he'd not had any major discipline problems, given that he found it difficult to be stern.

Friday arrived. This weekend was the choir picnic, and Todd had mixed feelings about it. On one hand, it was kind of the choir to have an event to welcome him. But with his introverted personality, socializing with a group of people he didn't know sent his pulse racing. At least Meg would be in attendance, so she would be a familiar friendly face.

Entering his apartment that afternoon, he released a long sigh. Maybe it was a blessing that he wasn't hosting Chip this weekend, because fatigue was taking over his body. Although his students hadn't been unruly, just being in charge of class after class each day took a toll. His phone rang, startling him.

His aunt's voice greeted him, asking about his week at school. Then she mentioned the choir picnic. "I think it's wonderful they're having a picnic to welcome you, Toddles. Don't worry about not knowing anyone. They're fine folks. You just relax and enjoy the picnic. Besides, that sweet Meg Mills will be there, so you can stay close to her." Ellen laughed lightly, but a coughing spell erupted, so the phone call came to a quick end.

As Todd fed Mozart and prepared a microwave meal for his supper, he thought about his aunt's advice to relax and enjoy the picnic. How he wished he could relax around a group that consisted mostly of strangers. Then he replayed his aunt's comment about Meg. *You can stay close to her.*

Thinking of his aunt's words brought a smile to his face. He would enjoy staying close to Meg, especially if it meant getting to know her better. Maybe this picnic wouldn't be so uncomfortable, after all.

~ ~ ~

"I'm so happy we have beautiful weather for our choir picnic, Zoey." Meg chattered happily as she and her friend rode together on Saturday morning. "Thanks again for driving. I hope I haven't forgotten anything." She'd gone over her list countless times, and even made a few reminder phone calls to choir members about the food they were bringing.

Zoey giggled. "It'll be great, so relax. I can tell you're a bit anxious about this." She kept her eyes on the road, but arched an eyebrow teasingly.

"I just want it to be nice so Todd feels welcome as our new choir director." Her friend had no doubt figured out that Meg was more than a little attracted to their future music leader.

"Well, I'm sure a picnic at Hidden Palms will make him feel welcome. Not to mention all the yummy food we'll have. Smelling the mac-and-cheese you made is driving me nuts. My stomach is already growling."

"I hope it'll taste good. I have no idea what

foods Todd likes, but with the assortment of side dishes and desserts, surely he won't leave hungry." A jittery giggle followed Meg's words. Could she really be nervous about being around Todd at the picnic? No, that was silly. She simply wanted him to feel welcomed since he would be leading their church choir.

Zoey's words cut into her thoughts. "Is Todd riding to the picnic with anyone?"

"No, I don't think so. He has directions to Hidden Palms, so he shouldn't have any trouble locating the area." She reached up and wiped a bit of moisture on her neck. Why hadn't she worn her hair up instead of leaving it loose on her shoulders? With the humidity, even in springtime, it was easy to become uncomfortable.

Minutes later Zoey pulled into a parking spot near the picnic pavilion, and the two women hopped out to unload the car. Meg had secretly hoped a couple of other choir members would already be there to help carry food to the picnic tables, but instead she and Zoey were the first to arrive. Great. With the humidity and her nervousness, she'd likely be dripping by the time the others arrived. *I want to look nice for Todd.* Yes, she couldn't deny it.

To Meg's relief, after carrying the first load of food to the pavilion, several other choir members arrived, quickly offering their assistance. Meg stayed under the pavilion roof, readying the tables. She set the food on one table, then spread red and white-checkered cloths on the other tables. She set out bright red paper napkins and disposable plates and cups.

Zoey added more side dishes to the food table. "Look what just arrived. I think we'll have plenty of food. And the table where we'll sit looks great, Meg. I think our new choir leader will feel very welcomed." She winked at Meg.

"Here's the guest of honor." One of the middle-aged ladies called out as Todd approached the pavilion. At the woman's announcement, he grinned sheepishly and ducked his head.

Why did she feel a tingle at seeing him? Meg knew she needed to rein in these feelings—at least in front of the others. This was a casual gathering to welcome their new leader and enjoy a time of fellowship.

Meg greeted Todd, and then each person introduced themselves, with a few people making jokes about trying not to sing off-key. Meg appreciated the choir members being so kind and welcoming.

Pastor Jack offered a blessing for their meal, then insisted that Todd go first in the food line.

Meg busied herself pouring iced tea into cups and making certain everyone had a place to sit. An early May breeze drifted through the pavilion now and then, which helped keep the temperature at a comfortable level, not to mention wafting the aroma of fried chicken through the air.

"You haven't even fixed your plate of food yet." One of the women playfully admonished Meg, insisting she eat right away. Minutes later, she headed to the table with her food, wondering where she'd sit.

Pastor Jack looked up and grinned at her.

"Here you go, Meg. You can sit right here." He had scooted a couple of feet along the picnic bench to allow room for her to sit—next to Todd.

As she lowered herself onto the bench, she hoped she'd be able to eat while sitting so close to him. A good bit of food remained on his plate. He must have been fielding questions from the choir members seated around him. Or, maybe he was too nervous to eat much.

"Do you need anything? Please get second helpings if you're still hungry. As you see, we have plenty of food." She gestured toward the table.

"Thanks, everything is really good." Todd nodded at her, then turned to the woman on his left, who asked a question about her piano.

Meg took a bite of green beans, but her mind had abruptly switched gears. What would it be like if she and Todd were a couple? Seated side-by-side at every event and activity they attended, talking to each other daily, and...kissing. Heat rushed up her face and she grabbed her cup of iced tea. *No daydreaming while I'm here.* She took another gulp of her tea, almost choking in the process.

Zoey had finished eating and was walking around snapping photos. After taking a few random shots, she directed her camera toward Meg and Todd, a playful look on her face. "Smile!" She instructed them before snapping several pictures.

Meg's face burned in embarrassment. Surely Todd wouldn't think she'd asked Zoey to take their photo together, would he? To keep the moment light, she laughed and wiped her mouth with her napkin. "I hope I didn't have chicken crumbs all over my face."

Todd grinned at her before focusing his attention on the pastor, who explained that the choir picnic photos would be displayed on the church bulletin board in the fellowship hall. Soon those who'd brought dishes began taking them to their cars. The pastor announced that it would be nice to walk to another area and continue their fellowship.

Meg walked beside Todd as the group left the pavilion area. "I'm so glad we've got beautiful weather today. If it had rained, we would've needed to reschedule our picnic."

"The food was great, and it's nice you all did this for me." Todd genuinely seemed to appreciate the picnic. He and Meg walked along a path behind other choir members. Trees surrounded them until they arrived at a clearing that offered a view of the lake.

Meg didn't miss the look of panic on Todd's face. Did he think they were planning to dive into the lake in their regular clothes? She chuckled and patted his arm. "Don't worry, we're not going swimming. Pastor Jack wanted us to have a different view as we continued visiting."

Todd had jerked his head away from looking at the lake, and now his eyes bore down on her. He appeared confused, as if not understanding what was going on.

Several of the men—including Pastor Jack—walked to the edge of the lake. Some of the women remained standing, but most sat on the wooden benches and swings placed in the clearing.

Zoey joined Meg and Todd and gestured

toward the lake. "Those men are so funny, trying to outdo each other with stories of their fishing adventures." She giggled, then looked up at Todd. "Do you like to fish?"

Todd offered a forced smile at Zoey, then shook his head.

Before Zoey could say more, another woman called to her with a question about a recipe, so she trotted over to the woman, leaving Meg and Todd standing by themselves.

"Would you like to sit?" Meg motioned to a nearby bench that had room for more.

Todd shook his head, ran a hand down his face, and in a lowered tone told her he needed to leave. "I-I don't feel well. Must've eaten too fast. Please tell everyone I appreciate the picnic." With that, he spun around and almost ran along the path toward the pavilion area.

Meg was stunned. What had just happened? A quick glance around let her know that apparently no one else had noticed the guest of honor making a hasty departure. Choir members were still clustered here and there, talking and laughing.

Zoey had finished discussing recipes, and now headed toward Meg. "Where's Todd?" She looked around.

"He just left—said he didn't feel well." Meg paused and drew in a deep breath. "He said he must've eaten too fast." She shook her head and shrugged.

A scowl formed on Zoey's face. "That's too bad. He looked like he was really enjoying himself at the picnic. And we wanted him to get to know our choir members, but he could only visit with those seated close to him during the meal."

"Yeah. That's the main purpose of this picnic today." Meg shook her head as worry poked at her. Suddenly the fried chicken she'd eaten earlier seemed to be a lead weight in her gut. Why had Todd rushed off so quickly? It had happened right after he'd had a good look at the lake, but that shouldn't make a person feel sick. It wasn't as though he'd dived into the water to swim laps around the lake.

In true Zoey form, her friend seemed to pick up on her worried thoughts, because she playfully jabbed Meg with her elbow. "Well, we might as well enjoy the pretty weather while we're here. Come on, let's socialize." She hooked an arm through Meg's.

Meg pasted on a smile as she walked with Zoey toward the lake. She'd analyze Todd's hasty departure later, because at the moment she needed to visit with the other choir members. *And pretend everything is fine.*

When she and Zoey joined a group standing by the lake, Pastor Jack immediately asked about Todd. "Did I see him heading toward the picnic pavilion?"

Before Meg could reply, Zoey spoke up. "Yes, he wasn't feeling well and had to leave. But I know he enjoyed the picnic." As the pastor and several others commented that it was too bad Todd got sick, Meg leaned toward Zoey and thanked her.

Thirty minutes later they headed back to Meg's cottage, the conversation more subdued. As hard as

Meg tried not to worry about Todd's quick exit, it was foremost on her mind.

Zoey chattered as she drove, mostly commenting on various dishes served at the picnic. Her friend was doing her best to distract her from thinking about Todd.

Yet at the back of her mind, Meg had a sneaking idea that she had been the cause of Todd's early exit from the picnic. Despite her good intentions in trying to be extra-friendly to him, she'd apparently been too friendly and talkative, driving him away.

How could she have ever thought she might be appealing to Todd? They were polar opposites, and it didn't matter what the old saying was about opposites attracting, because she had driven him further away.

~ ~ ~

What had he done? Todd could've kicked himself after reaching his car near the pavilion. Maybe he should've kept his eyes off the lake and instead focused on the people. Mainly Meg. She probably thought he was nuts. After all, he'd been fine one minute, then suddenly he mumbled about feeling sick and almost ran away from the group.

But when he had seen the lake, it instantly brought back the panic from years ago. Gasping for air. Knowing he was going to drown. And the painful memories of Earl's taunts as he shoved Todd's head underwater. *I'm thirty-two years old, not a little kid.* Shouldn't he have gotten over that horrible time in his life by now?

Even if Meg now thought he was crazy, hopefully the entire choir wasn't aware of his odd behavior when he left the picnic. If so, the church would likely be searching for someone else to lead their choir.

After leaving Hidden Palms park, Todd drove numbly to the Coastal Breeze community, and on a whim decided to visit his aunt. *If* she happened to be home. Knowing the social butterfly she was, it was likely that Aunt Ellen was shopping with some of her friends. Then again, since she wasn't completely over her cough yet, maybe she'd be home.

Ellen greeted Todd at her front door, happy but surprised to see him. "Why Toddles, was the choir picnic cancelled today? The weather is beautiful." A confused shadow flitted over her face.

Although he was always relaxed with his aunt, Todd cringed. There was no way he would ever lie to Aunt Ellen, so he may as well explain what had happened. He ran a hand down his face and drew in a deep breath.

"The picnic was very nice. The choir made me feel welcomed, and they acted as though they're really glad I'll be their new leader. The food was great, and as you said—the weather today is beautiful." He paused, noting the concern growing in his aunt's eyes.

"So…what was the problem? Surely the picnic lasted longer than an hour." Ellen's voice was barely above a whisper.

Of course, for Todd it had been terrible—at the

time. The sudden onset of sheer panic had gripped him, and he'd had no choice but to leave. At least that's what he told himself.

"We left the pavilion area and headed to a clearing in the woods. It seemed nice, with benches and swings. But then on past that area I could see the lake." He shook his head. "For a few seconds, looking at that lake brought back the memories of—" He didn't want to say his cousin's name, but Ellen knew that Earl had been less than kind to Todd when they were younger.

Ellen reached out and patted his arm. "Your horrible memories of being in the lake with Earl resurfaced today, didn't they?" The understanding and kindness in his aunt's eyes almost brought tears. What would he do without this precious relative in his life?

"Yes, and now it sounds so ridiculous and silly. But at the time, it was awful. Being that close to a lake that looked so much like the lake we visited when I was a kid…it was just too much."

Ellen insisted that Todd sit at her kitchen table, then she poured him a glass of iced tea. In her soothing voice she offered words of wisdom. "Toddles, I really think that the fact Earl has been in the area recently has triggered these horrible memories for you. Now I'm certainly no psychologist or know a lot about how our brains work, but I truly feel that's why being near the lake today affected you that way."

Her words made him feel better already. She hadn't belittled him or minimized his fear. He thanked her and offered to run any errands for her while he was out. After she insisted she didn't need a thing, their visit continued a few more minutes. But when a coughing spell started, Todd knew she needed to rest, so he hugged her good-bye.

"Thanks for making me feel better, Aunt Ellen. Remember, if you need anything, please phone me. If your cough continues, you might not need to attend church tomorrow." He suppressed a grin. Ellen had to be extremely ill to miss a church service.

Driving to his apartment a few minutes later, Todd allowed his mind to think about the friendly choir members he'd met at the picnic. That part of his day had been good—until the group had walked to a different area of the park and he'd glimpsed the lake.

Yet, as he replayed his aunt's words about Earl's recent presence dredging up the painful memories, Todd felt certain she was right. Maybe he wasn't crazy after all, as he'd felt when leaving the Hidden Palms Park earlier. If only he'd not been with Meg when he panicked. The look on her face was one he couldn't forget. Not only puzzled, but hurt.

8

Meg hadn't spoken with Todd after church the next day. She'd seen him sitting with his sweet aunt in the congregation, but after the service she and Zoey chatted before heading to their cars, and Todd had already left. That was fine because after his hasty departure from the picnic the previous day, she still wondered what was going on.

Although he'd told her he felt sick, Meg still found it strange how suddenly he bolted. As much as she tried to tamp down negative thoughts, she couldn't help it. If she'd just not been so overbearing, he wouldn't have fled. Maybe he'd decided the only way to escape was to act sick. Or was she being ridiculous?

One thing was certain—she had a lot of work to do. Finishing her job at Dr. Phipps's office in addition to preparing her bookstore didn't leave much time for worrying about other matters. Dr. Phipps had hired another office manager and asked if Meg would help train her before leaving. Of course, she graciously agreed to train the new employee.

At choir practice on Wednesday evening, several choir members asked Meg if Todd enjoyed the picnic, since he'd left abruptly. She assured them he did and offered the explanation he'd given her of not feeling well. One of the older ladies in the choir commented that she hoped his sickness wasn't from any of the dishes they'd prepared.

"Oh, I really don't think so. He probably just ate too quickly." She smiled at the lady, hoping her comments were convincing. Now if Meg could only convince herself that she wasn't the cause of Todd's abrupt departure from the picnic.

On Saturday, Meg was in her store by nine o'clock that morning, eager to make progress on her business. The evening before, her father had brought several bookcases that relatives had donated, along with three more boxes of books. Excitement mingled with nervousness as Meg surveyed the empty bookcases and boxes sitting here and there.

Her dad had offered to return Saturday to help her, but he'd already done so much. Besides, Zoey had assured her she'd arrive around noon to work all afternoon, so surely between the two of them the store would start taking shape.

Meg was sorting through one of the boxes, taking out the books for children, when a sudden tap on her glass door caused her to drop a book. With shaking hands, she retrieved the book and glanced toward the door. Todd. What was he doing here?

She headed to unlock the door and invite him inside. His hands were stuffed in his pockets, and he barely made eye contact with her.

"Hi, Todd. This is a surprise." She smiled, wanting to sound polite but still reminded of how he'd fled the picnic. A silent voice warned her to guard her heart.

"I'm sorry to stop by unannounced, but since I'd offered to help you unpack boxes, I thought I'd better check and see if you could still use some help."

Meg gestured to the boxes placed at various spots, all waiting to be unpacked and sorted. Not to mention getting them onto shelves. "I guess it's obvious what my answer would be." She laughed. "Are you sure you have time? It's Saturday and you must have better things to do." She grinned up at him, even more aware of his good looks. Her pulse quickened.

He nodded at her and then shrugged. "I don't have any piano tuning jobs today, and my aunt doesn't need me to do work at her house, so yes. I've got time." He offered a slight grin, appearing a bit embarrassed.

"Then great. But please feel free to leave when you need to, because I know this isn't exciting work." She gestured to a nearby box and explained her sorting process. "I plan to have things arranged more attractively before the store opens for business, but for now I'm just trying to sort the books into genres. Books for children on this shelf, nonfiction here, adult romance here, and everything else goes on this shelf for now."

"Okay, sounds good." He opened a box and got to work.

Meg hoped things wouldn't be awkward with just the two of them working in such close proximity to each other, but Zoey would be arriving at noon.

She needn't have worried, though, because the time passed quickly. Meg purposely didn't mention his hasty exit from the choir picnic, but at one point she asked if he was feeling better. When he appeared puzzled, she explained. "Last Saturday at the picnic, you weren't feeling well, so I was hoping if you had a virus, it didn't last long."

A blush covered his face as he ducked his head. Then he raised his gaze and nodded. "I'm okay, thanks for asking."

It was obvious he didn't want to discuss the matter, so Meg didn't push. Instead she questioned him about his substitute teaching job, and that question led to an amusing conversation about his students. "I have to admit I've enjoyed the position more than I'd expected to, but I wouldn't want to teach full-time."

About eleven o'clock, Meg's cell phone rang, showing a call from Zoey. As soon as she heard her friend's voice, her heart sank. Zoey was battling a migraine and would be unable to help her that day. "I'm so sorry you're dealing with a horrible headache, but you don't worry. You just take care of yourself. Do I need to bring you anything?" Zoey thanked her and assured her she had everything she needed.

When Meg clicked off her phone, she quickly explained the call to Todd, hoping he hadn't noticed that she'd not mentioned his presence to her friend.

She planned to tell Zoey about Todd helping her, but didn't want to keep her friend on the phone any longer than necessary.

"Poor Zoey sounded miserable. Thankfully she doesn't get migraines often, but when she does, it's a killer."

Sympathy filled Todd's gaze as he shook his head. "That must be terrible. I'm glad I don't have them. From what I've heard, they can be really miserable."

The pair continued unpacking and sorting books, with an occasional comment about certain ones. Thirty minutes later, Meg was about to remind Todd that he could leave at any time, when he surprised her.

"Uh, would you like to go somewhere and eat?"

Her eyes widened, but she didn't want him to know how unexpected this was, so she pasted on a smile and nodded. "That would be great. To be honest, I hadn't really thought about food for today, but I've got some crackers in my bag." She giggled. "I guess you need more than that."

At that moment, a strange look covered Todd's face as he gazed out the glass storefront. He turned to Meg and reached out to grab her arm. "Come on. We need to hide."

~ ~ ~

Of all the times to see Earl ambling along the street, why did it have to be now? Todd's heart raced. He ushered Meg to the small back room of her store. If she didn't already think he was nuts, she certainly would now. He'd need to explain, yet he was reluctant to share many details about his cousin.

Things had been going so well while they'd worked side-by-side that morning. And now he was about to take her out to lunch. That is, until he noticed Earl outside the bookstore. He'd recognized him immediately. Why hadn't Earl returned to Kentucky? Deep down, Todd knew the answer. His seedy cousin still hoped to weasel money from Ellen.

Meg was peering up at him, eyebrows furrowed over her blue eyes. "What's going on? Who are we hiding from?"

Todd released her arm and felt more than a little foolish. "I'm so sorry, Meg. But I saw my cousin Earl heading down the street, and if he saw us, he'd be sure to stop." What a predicament. He shook his head and thrust his hands into the pockets of his jeans. "He has some…issues, including substance abuse. My aunt and I were hoping he'd returned to Kentucky, where he lives."

"Do you think he was looking for you? How would he even know you might be here?"

Todd shrugged. "No, he'd have no reason to know I'm here. He's probably just out looking around. But it would be best if he didn't see me." He must sound pathetic, hiding from a cousin. Yet he had to hope Meg would understand, even if she didn't know all the facts about Earl and their past.

Todd was struck with another thought. He had parked in one of the parallel spots along the street.

Would his cousin remember the kind of car he drove?

"What is it? You look more worried now." Meg was standing mere inches away studying his face. Even after working with musty books all morning, she still had a fresh, floral scent about her.

He released a sigh. "I was just hoping Earl won't remember what my car looks like. I parked on the street by Cindy Lou's Candy Shop."

Meg reached out and patted his arm, then offered a reassuring grin. "He probably won't."

Todd appreciated her support, yet was sure she was only saying that to help ease his obvious anxiety at the moment. Another thought jolted him. He needed to let his aunt know he'd seen Earl walking along this street. With Coastal Breeze being a small community, it was easy to walk from the shopping area to the residential section.

He explained to Meg that he needed to phone his aunt, and then if he didn't spot his cousin, they'd get in his car and go to eat. Ellen answered on the second ring, assuring him she was fine and reminding him that Earl had no idea of her address.

When the call ended, he released a sigh. "Okay, if we don't see him, we'll head to my car. I'm so sorry about this." He knew Meg's mind must be full of questions, but right now he only wanted to get to a restaurant and spend time with her.

Once inside his car, Todd glanced at Meg and asked where she'd like to eat. When she replied anywhere was good, he decided on a whim to head to The Happy Fisherman. They were both dressed casually, but that was fine for a Saturday lunch.

No sign of Earl as Todd drove the short distance to the restaurant, and he felt pretty safe in assuming his wayward cousin wouldn't be entering this eating establishment today—at least he prayed that wouldn't happen. He had to shove that thought from his mind and focus on making the most of this outing with the pretty Meg Mills. Would she consider this a date?

Her presence walking beside him took his mind away from worries about Earl. Todd held the door for her. The restaurant wasn't too crowded. Good. He requested a booth toward the back, and the hostess happily obliged.

"Please order anything you'd like—this is my treat." Good thing he'd made sure to stop by the bank this past week so he had some cash in his wallet. He tried to limit using his credit card when possible.

Meg giggled. "That's so sweet, but since you're helping me work in my bookstore, I should be treating you." The look she sent him almost made Todd's mind go blank. Her eyes reminded Todd of the ocean at certain times—how could she look so pretty after unpacking musty boxes all morning?

"No, I insist." *And maybe you'll even consider this a date.* That thought sent a warmth rushing to his face, so Todd grabbed his water and took a swig.

After placing their orders, Todd owed Meg an explanation about his cousin. As much as he didn't want to spend their time together discussing Earl, he felt he must. But he wouldn't share everything—just enough details to enlighten Meg about Earl's substance abuse and the family's concerns. No need to tell her how his cousin had tormented him when they were much younger.

With kindness and understanding evident in her gaze, Meg listened intently as Todd gave a brief overview of his cousin, adding how surprised he and his aunt had been to discover Earl was in the area, rather than in Kentucky.

"Why do you think he came all the way to the Florida panhandle from Kentucky?" Meg asked, then peered at him over the top of her water glass.

Todd shook his head. "As much as I hate sharing this, my gut feeling is that Earl hopes our Aunt Ellen will take pity on him, and help him financially. Which she would, except she's certain he'd squander the money on alcohol and who knows what else. It's really sad."

Meg reached across the table and gently patted his arm, as she'd done earlier when they were hiding in her store. "I'm sorry about this situation, and I'll add your cousin to my prayer list. But don't be embarrassed over someone you can't control. Most families have a relative or two that causes concern."

At that moment, their server arrived with their meals. Now that she knew the truth, Todd could actually enjoy his food—and the lovely lady seated across from him.

What surprised Todd the most was how comfortable he was beginning to feel around Meg. Rather than viewing her as an attractive, outgoing woman who'd have no interest in someone like himself, he now saw her as a very caring person, who appeared to be enjoying his company today.

Could this be the beginning of a real relationship with Meg? After all, they were so opposite in personality. But as their conversation continued during the meal, and then later in the bookstore while they worked, Todd's heart felt lighter than it had in a long time. And for that, he was very thankful.

~ ~ ~

When Todd returned to his apartment about five o'clock that afternoon, his heart was as light as the breeze outside. His time with Meg had gone very well, and she'd been so appreciative of his help. Except for the hiding incident when he saw Earl on the street, the day had been perfect.

He'd been able to casually mention the possibility of going out in the near future, and Meg was agreeable. In fact, Todd had been pleasantly shocked at the look of delight on her pretty face when he'd mentioned it. Finally, things seemed to be looking up in his life. Now, if he could find a few students for private music lessons, he'd be financially secure for the foreseeable future. Certainly not wealthy, but he'd be able to purchase a house for himself and Mozart.

Feeling a bit restless, Todd decided on a quick walk on the beach while there was still daylight. Since it was May, the days were getting longer, so he wanted to take advantage of the sunshine.

Only a handful of beachgoers strolled on the sand when Todd arrived, and several of those appeared to be heading to the parking lot to leave. That was fine with him—he preferred the empty space with no distractions—only the calls of the seagulls and the pounding surf—at a distance—since he stayed away from the water.

As he breathed in the salty air, his mind took off. This had been the weekend his buddy Chip Ledbetter was supposed to visit, but when Chip's wife and toddler both caught a virus, the visit was cancelled. Although disappointed at first, Todd made the most of the change in plans, and spent the day helping Meg.

The sun was beginning to sink and the earlier bright rays were dimming. Todd was the only person remaining on the beach, except for a couple further down, and one man who headed toward the water. Todd hadn't noticed the man earlier, so he must've just arrived. He was staggering, obviously unsteady on his feet. Was he drunk? The man continued toward the water's edge.

Todd stopped walking to see what the man would do. Surely he wouldn't go into the water, would he? Looking in both directions, Todd saw that no one else remained on the beach—except for the older couple holding hands who came toward him. They must be heading to the parking lot to leave. Apparently, they didn't notice the man because they continued talking and laughing, eyes only for each other.

As though frozen to the spot, Todd watched in horror as the unsteady man entered the water. High tide was coming in, and the waves were becoming bigger and stronger. With his unstable movements, the man was no match for the ocean. A powerful wave knocked him over, and his hands flailed about. Would he be able to pull himself out of the water?

Todd knew in that moment that he must do something to help this stranger. But could he enter the water's edge? Could he pull the man from the pounding surf? He had to. Ignoring his fears, Todd ran toward the ocean just as the man went down again. Now completely underwater, the man didn't appear to be making any moves to get above the water. Had he given up? Or was he under the influence of something that had limited his movements—along with his thinking? Or had an undertow overpowered him?

Lord, I can't do this alone. I need Your help. Running into the ocean, Todd grabbed the stranger by an arm to pull him above the water. He could not let him drown. The man fought him off, flailing his arms. As Todd tightened his hold on the man's arm and fought his way to the shore, Todd got a better look at the man. This was no stranger—this was his cousin.

"Come on, Earl. You need to get out of the water." Todd wasn't sure if Earl even heard him, but he spoke the words anyway. His cousin's stocky build, combined with the weight of wet clothing, made it challenging for Todd to pull him from the grip of the ocean. But sheer adrenaline helped him drag Earl out of the water, and now his cousin lay sprawled on the wet sand.

The older couple joined him. "What happened?" The woman questioned Todd. Ginny, the lady who ran the gift shop. The man beside her clutched his cell phone.

Earl's eyes were closed, and he was still sprawled on the wet sand. Todd called his name, then checked his airways. Though unresponsive, he was breathing.

Todd looked at the older couple, trying to control his shaking hands. "This is my cousin Earl...from Kentucky...Don't know why he entered the water." Todd's breath was still ragged.

Ginny beamed and patted Todd's arm. "Well, you just saved your cousin's life. If you hadn't pulled him from the ocean, the undertow would've pulled him under."

She turned to the man behind her. "This is my husband, Claude Grover. You've probably seen him at church." He shook hands with Todd.

"I've called for an ambulance, so they should arrive soon. When I saw what was happening, I thought it best to call." Claude's voice was solemn.

Todd thanked him and drew in another ragged breath. This entire scene was surreal. Conversing on the beach with the Grovers after pulling Earl from the ocean—surely this must be a dream. Yet as the siren's wail came closer and the ambulance stopped in the parking area, Todd knew this was real.

He had saved the life of the same cousin who'd tormented him in his youth. The cousin who'd taunted him and made him feel inferior. By the grace of God, Todd had actually entered the water—the pounding, powerful surf—and pulled his cousin to safety. Just as he freed Earl from the grasp of the tide, Todd knew his memories no longer had a grasp on him.

~ ~ ~

"This is so exciting." Zoey squealed and spun in a circle in Meg's almost-completed bookstore. "You'll have your grand opening in only two more weeks."

Meg beamed. "Yep, I feel like I'm dreaming. The third Saturday in June I'll officially be open for business. Just a few more details to take care of for opening day, mainly getting refreshments ready to serve." She giggled, then gazed up at Todd, feeling a warmth rush through her.

"Remember, my Aunt Ellen and I are providing food. She insists on baking cookies and I'll buy the drinks." He placed an arm around Meg's shoulder. "Everything will be fine."

Meg fought a wave of emotion as she stared at Todd and Zoey. "I couldn't have done all this without both of you." They'd offered many hours of help the past two weeks.

"And now you don't have Cruella bothering you with annoying phone calls, since Roy's cousin told you she'd remarried and moved up north." Zoey giggled.

Todd wore a puzzled frown and looked at both women. "Cruella?"

Meg patted his arm. "I'll explain later. But Zoey, you're right. When Roy's cousin phoned me and told me the news, I was ready to celebrate."

Zoey looked at Todd. "So how does it feel to be the hero of Coastal Breeze? After saving your cousin from drowning, tons of people are talking about what a wonderful thing you did."

A crimson hue covered Todd's face and he shrugged. "I'm no hero." His humble comment was quickly followed by opposition from the two women, who argued that he most definitely qualified as a hero.

Noticing how embarrassed Todd appeared, Meg moved the topic to Earl. "How's your cousin doing now? Is he back in Kentucky?"

"Yes, his parents—my aunt and uncle—drove down to get him. The car Earl had was in bad shape, so they sold it and took him home to Kentucky, where he's currently in a rehab program for substance abuse." Todd paused and shook his head. "Really sad, but we're all praying this treatment helps him." After a few beats of silence, he continued. "I never thought Earl would've attempted to end his life, but apparently his drug and alcohol problems got the better of him. I'm thankful that he and I were able to talk briefly, before his parents drove him back to Kentucky. He actually apologized for bullying me when we were younger."

The women nodded solemnly, then Meg spoke up. "After you shared with me how Earl had treated you in the past, it's wonderful you ended up rescuing him." Not wanting to further embarrass Todd, she giggled. "Ginny brags on you to her customers in the gift shop. She's also proud that her husband phoned for the ambulance."

After visiting a few more minutes, Zoey headed to the door. "If you're sure there's nothing else I need to do, I'll go and get ready for my date with Trevor this evening." She flashed an exuberant smile.

Meg was thrilled that Zoey's boyfriend had finally gotten serious about their relationship. "Don't forget that we're going to have a double-date with you and Trevor before long." She reached out and took Todd's hand, feeling that same tingle she'd experienced when looking at him from afar. After he'd helped her the first time in her store, the couple had begun dating, and she couldn't be happier. From all indications, Todd was happy too.

The couple had discussed their opposite personalities, but had decided that together they made a good pair. Meg credited Todd's work as the choir director with gradually helping him to be less introverted, while she tried not to overwhelm him with her outgoing mannerisms. She was relieved when he told her that he admired her friendliness, and he even admitted that was one trait that had drawn him to her.

An hour later, the couple sat at Ellen's kitchen table, enjoying a lunch of her tasty tuna salad. It was obvious that she was thrilled her nephew and Meg were officially dating now.

"Miss Ellen, your tuna salad is yummy. I enjoy making it, but I think your recipe is better than mine. Come to think of it, I was making tuna salad the day I met Todd, when he tuned my piano."

Beaming, Ellen winked at the couple. "I'll gladly give you my recipe, dear. Which reminds me—have you heard the joke that says you can tune a piano, but you can't tuna fish?"

They all burst out laughing, and Todd reached for Meg's hand under the table. She wrapped her fingers around his, and with a grateful heart looked forward to many more dates with her handsome piano tuner.

EPILOGUE

"Okay, folks. Let's go over our Christmas cantata music one more time, then we'll call it a night." Todd gazed out at the faces smiling up at him. He'd been the church choir director since June and was loving every minute. More members had joined the choir, and everyone seemed eager to perform the special music selections Todd had chosen. Of course, Aunt Ellen couldn't be prouder of her nephew, and was especially pleased that he and Meg had a future together.

Meg grinned at Zoey, who was admiring the diamond ring Trevor had given her at Thanksgiving. Then Meg admired her own sparkling ring, and thoughts of her upcoming January wedding with Todd filled her mind. Yet she needed to stay focused on Christmas first—not only practicing for the choir cantata, but also planning special activities in her bookstore, which had been a welcomed addition to Coastal Breeze. Sometimes she still thought she was dreaming when she stood in her small store and gazed at shelves filled with books, in addition to a special area for children.

As she joined with the others in singing, Meg's heart was filled with love for Todd. Watching him direct the choir, his long arms moving in time to the music, she could tell he genuinely loved this job. Actually, he loved anything to do with music, including tuning pianos. Tuning jobs lined up, in addition to local residents who'd asked him to give private lessons on the piano.

What made Meg's heart smile the most was knowing that above all, Todd loved her and wanted to spend time with her. He had assured her that since none of his other jobs required a full-time commitment, he planned to also help in her bookstore.

Meg knew they'd have a happy, blessed life together after their winter wedding the following month. Their life would be filled with music, books, and cats. After the wedding, Todd and Mozart would move into Meg's house. The couple also hoped to be blessed with children one day, and Meg's heart danced with thoughts of being a wife and mother.

As the choir practiced the final number for the cantata, Meg gazed lovingly at the choir director. So much had happened since March—in a matter of months, her whole life had changed. The Lord had certainly brought music into her life—in the form of a very handsome piano tuner. And she couldn't be happier.

The End

After teaching the first grade and kindergarten for 21 years, Patti Jo had to retire early due to severe spinal problems. She saw this as an opportunity to fulfill her dream of writing full-time, which she loves. A life-long Georgia girl, Patti Jo loves Jesus, her family, and cats. The Lord blessed her abundantly this year with her very first grandbaby and her first writing contract. She's excited about being a Forget-Me-Not Author, and is looking forward to connecting with lots of readers.

www.ingramcontent.com/pod-product-compliance
Lightning Source LLC
LaVergne TN
LVHW012019060526
838201LV00061B/4371